W9-BKB-675

Estelle Oldham at the time of her engagement to Cornell Franklin in April 1918. Courtesy Jill Faulkner Summers.

VISION IN SPRING

WILLIAM FAULKNER

Vision in Spring

With an Introduction by Judith L. Sensibar

UNIVERSITY OF TEXAS PRESS, AUSTIN

Printed in the United States of America

First Edition, 1984
First printing, March 1984
Second printing, April 1984

LIBRARY OF CONGRESS
CATALOGING IN PUBLICATION DATA

Faulkner, William, 1897–1962.
Vision in spring.

I. Title.
PS3511.A86V57 1984 811'.52 83-21888
ISBN 0-292-78712-X

CONTENTS

An unused publicity photograph of William Faulkner in 1924 taken shortly before publication of The Marble Faun.

Courtesy Jill Faulkner Summers.

ACKNOWLEDGMENTS

Grateful acknowledgment is made to the following:

Jill Faulkner Summers, for permission to print William Faulkner's *Vision in Spring* and other unpublished and published poems and fragments and for providing the photographs of her parents, William Faulkner and Estelle Oldham Faulkner.

The University of Texas, for permission to publish materials from the William Faulkner Collection at the Humanities Research Center, University of Texas at Austin.

Random House, Inc., for permission to include *Vision in Spring* XI and XIII, which, with slight variants, were first published in William Faulkner's *A Green Bough* (1933).

Keen Butterworth and the *Mississippi Quarterly*, for permission to include material from "A Census of Manuscripts and Typescripts of William Faulkner's Poetry," *Mississippi Quarterly* 26 (Summer 1973): 333–359.

The American Council of Learned Societies, and the National Endowment for the Humanities, for a fellowship (Recent Recipients of the Ph.D., 1983–84).

VISION IN SPRING

WILLIAM FAULKNER

Photocopy of the cover of William Faulkner's Vision in Spring.

Introduction to *Vision in Spring*

IN LONDON in May 1921, T. S. Eliot began writing the poem sequence that most would agree became the "classic, and controversial, poem of the Modernist movement."[1] In Oxford, Mississippi, that same spring William Faulkner was completing a sequence of poems that, though he never published it, would prove revolutionary to his own development. *Vision in Spring*, the pivotal work in Faulkner's self-apprenticeship, is an eighty-eight–page, purple ribbon, carbon typescript, which he first hand bound that summer.[2] Read in the context of his other poetry, his life, and both his early and his best novels, this cycle of fourteen poems reveals fascinating information about how, during this apparently unrewarding period when he wrote poetry almost exclusively (ca. 1916 to 1924), the young Faulkner taught himself to write. It also suggests the myriad ways in which his poetry in general and this sequence in particular inform the intention, the mode, and the moral preoccupations of his great fiction. As these issues are treated in detail elsewhere, I will only suggest general areas of importance here.[3]

Vision in Spring, first noted in Joseph Blotner's biography, is the sixth of Faulkner's handmade books to be published since his death in 1962 and the third complete and most ambitious of all his extant early poem sequences. Given to his future wife, Estelle Franklin, in 1921 and owned by her until her death in 1972, the original has apparently disappeared. A photocopy of it, missing the fourth and fifth pages, was recently recovered from among some unsorted papers owned by Faulkner's daughter, Jill Faulkner Summers.[4]

---

1. See David Perkins' discussion of *The Waste Land* in *A History of Modern Poetry from the 1890s to the High Modernist Mode* (Cambridge, Mass.: Harvard University Press, 1976), p. 498.
2. For a description of the original volume, see Joseph Blotner, *Faulkner, A Biography*, vol. I (New York: Random House, 1974), pp. 307–312 and revised edition (1984), pp. 96–98. "The typescript itself, including Title page and Contents page is 91 pp. The entire booklet, including all unnumbered pages, is 99 pp." (Joseph Blotner, letter, 14 June 1983).
3. See Judith L. Sensibar, *The Origins of Faulkner's Art* (Austin: University of Texas Press, 1984). This book treats in detail three major poem sequences from a series Faulkner wrote before beginning his first novel in 1925. It discusses in their context related lyrics and Faulkner's 1920 dream-play *The Marionettes*. These works demarcate the essence—aesthetic and psychological—of Faulkner's self-designed poetic apprenticeship. Faulkner's poetry was essential to the development of his narrative style. His assumption of the intriguing Pierrot mask and his early and ever-increasing commitment to cyclical arrangements of his poetry prepared the way for the multilayered structures of his greatest fiction. For a fascinating discussion of the "dramatic and psychological types" Pierrot embodied and his importance to the Modernists, see Robert F. Storey, *Pierrot: A Critical History of a Mask* (Princeton: Princeton University Press, 1978).
4. This photocopy of *Vision in Spring* (missing pages 4 and 5) is in Jill Faulkner Summers' private collection. Shortly before *Vision in Spring* was to go to press additional information about the original manuscript became available. I am indebted to Joseph Blotner for supplying photocopies of the missing fourth and fifth pages and other facts concerning the physical condition of the original manuscript.

To date Faulkner's other known complete sequences are *The Lilacs* (January 1920); an early unpublished typescript version of *The Marble Faun* (some poems in it are dated 1920); a manuscript, now lost, that may have been a revision of *Vision in Spring* called *Orpheus, and Other Poems* (1923); and *Helen: A Courtship* (June 1926). Incomplete sequences are the first seven of the *Mississippi Poems* (1924) and seven of the fifteen "Aunt Bama Poems" (ca. 1917).[5] Examination of all available and extant Faulkner poetry indicates the existence of other sequence fragments as well.

Blotner, the only scholar to have seen and written about the unique and original copy of *Vision in Spring*, describes it as a 5½ × 8–inch hardcover book bound in "brownish-green mottled paper. On a small square of white linen paper in the upper right hand corner [of the cover] in India ink he had lettered the title, *Vision in Spring*, and his name" (see photocopy of cover and Appendix A). *Vision* looks as if it were meant to be commercially published. Faulkner has not decorated his text with anything that might distract the reader from its language. Typescript replaces the ornate hand lettering of *The Lilacs*, *The Marionettes*, and other booklets. *Vision*'s title page, on which he typed publication information ("Manuscript Edition. 1921.") is followed by a paginated table of contents, then the opening poem. Each page of poetry is numbered at the bottom.[6] The poems occupy pages 1 through 88. Front and back matter are unnumbered. The binding, as Blotner notes, is a rebinding. On unnumbered page 89, opposite the last page of verse, Faulkner has printed in black ink, "REBOUND 26 JANUARY 1926. OXFORD, MISSISSIPPI." Other than its hand-lettered title, this is the only holograph writing on *Vision in Spring*. While Blotner and Summers agree that none of the markings on the typescript itself are Faulkner's, Blotner says that Estelle Faulkner underlined in pencil phrases or lines she liked and that the insertions and deletions belong to an unknown friend or editor. Summers says that none of the handwriting on the typescript is her mother's.[7]

---

5. For information on *Orpheus*, see Blotner, *Faulkner*, pp. 349, 350 and rev. ed., pp. 113–114; and Joseph Blotner, ed., *Selected Letters of William Faulkner* (New York: Random House, 1977), pp. 5–6. For the *Mississippi Poems* and *Helen: A Courtship*, see William Faulkner, *Helen: A Courtship and Mississippi Poems*, ed. Carvel Collins and Joseph Blotner (Oxford: Yoknapatawpha Press, and New Orleans: Tulane University, 1981). For bibliographic descriptions of *The Lilacs* and sequential sections of "The Aunt Bama Poems" and the *Mississippi Poems*, see Louis Daniel Brodsky and Robert W. Hamblin, *Faulkner: A Comprehensive Guide to the Brodsky Collection* (Jackson: University Press of Mississippi, 1982), #26, #18 a–g, and #45 a–g.
6. Poems in Faulkner's other extant sequences and sequence fragments are often identified by a roman numeral and/or a title with pagination at bottom. For examples, see note 5 and fragments in Faulkner collections at the University of Virginia; the Humanities Research Center, University of Texas at Austin; and private collections of L. D. Brodsky and Leila Clark Wynn. Numbering on the *Mississippi Poems* and "The Aunt Bama Poems" was first noted by James B. Meriwether in *The Literary Career of William Faulkner: A Bibliographical Study* (Princeton: Princeton University Library, 1961).
7. Joseph Blotner, phone conversation, 1 June 1983, and letter, 4 June 1983; Jill Faulkner Summers, interview, 29 July 1980.

Those familiar with Faulkner's handmade books dating from the early 1920s will recognize in this description similarities to the bindings of at least two other extant unique volumes. *Mayday*, Faulkner's 1926 fable, and *Helen: A Courtship* were also bound with what look like handpainted mottled covers. The colors on *Mayday* were underwater greens, greys, and steely blues shot through with iridescent gold and silver, while *Helen*'s tones were blues, deep purples, rusts and rosy rusts, greys, and pale pinks flecked with gold leaf. Judging from what is known of Faulkner's skills as an artist and watercolorist it seems likely that he painted as well as fitted all three covers.

While its binding connects *Vision in Spring* with these other volumes, the physical appearance of its text sharply differentiates it. Its paginated table of contents, its impersonal typescript, the absence of a dedication, and the notation on its title page all suggest that Faulkner had a larger audience in mind. In June 1923 he did submit for publication what was apparently a revision of this sequence retitled *Orpheus, and Other Poems* to the Four Seas Company. As far as is known, *Orpheus* was the first full-length book manuscript Faulkner ever submitted to a publisher. Although it too seems to have disappeared, fragments of a sequence similar to *Vision in Spring* are included in the Faulkner Collection of the Humanities Research Center at the University of Texas at Austin (for examples see Appendix B). Also in that collection are slightly altered versions of *Vision* poems, some of which have been assigned different numbers.

Faulkner probably chose the Four Seas Company in part because it had published the majority of Conrad Aiken's early sequences, many of which he had read and several of which he mentioned in his admiring 1921 review of Aiken's *Turns and Movies and Other Tales in Verse*. In fact, lines appearing in *Vision in Spring* are typed on a holograph penciled draft of this review.[8] Anyone familiar with what Aiken called his "symphonies in verse" will hear them resonating throughout *Vision in Spring*. Although Four Seas offered Faulkner essentially the same publishing terms for *Orpheus* that he would accept a little more than six months later for *The Marble Faun*, Faulkner wrote a sardonic and somewhat bitter reply turning them down: "As I have no money I cannot very well guarantee the initial cost of publishing this mss.; besides, on re-reading some of the things, I see they aren't particularly significant and one may obtain no end of poor verse at a dollar and twenty-five cents a volume" (23 November 1923).[9]

As he did with his later sequences and would do with material from his short stories and novels, Faulkner reused poems from *Vision* in other cycles and also published some separately. "Portrait" (*VIS* V) was published in *The Double Dealer* (June

8. See Sensibar, *Origins*, figure 8; for a discussion of Aiken's, Eliot's, and other Modernists' roles in Faulkner's poetic apprenticeship, see *Origins*, chaps. 7, 10.
9. Blotner, *Selected Letters*, p. 6. For a discussion and explanation of Faulkner's turnabout, see Sensibar, *Origins*, chap. 12.

1922) and the sequence's title poem ("Vision in Spring") and its final poem ("April") appeared in a 1932 issue of *Contempo* devoted to Faulkner's work (*Contempo* 1, no. 17 [1 February 1932]). Faulkner included versions of the eleventh and thirteenth poems in *A Green Bough* (1933). Thus nine of the fourteen poems that constitute *Vision in Spring* are published here for the first time.[10]

THE BACKGROUND

Between the ages of about sixteen and twenty-seven Faulkner composed and revised hundreds of poems. As Keen Butterworth's census shows, Faulkner reworked many of his poems.[11] The census, valuable though it is, could not include all of Faulkner's poetry. Poems and fragments of poem sequences owned by private collectors were not then and are not now available for cataloging. Other poetry has either been lost or destroyed.[12] Both the sheer volume of work and the long time he spent as a poet demand that we not dismiss this work as juvenilia, the work "of a young romantic . . . losing himself in a baseless dreamworld."[13] He was, after all, not so very young: about twenty-four when he wrote *Vision* and twenty-seven when he completed and published *The Marble Faun*.

Faulkner's individual poems seem far removed from his fiction, even from his first novel, *Soldiers' Pay*. But at least by 1920 and probably even earlier, Faulkner was also working with a much more expansive formal structure: the poem sequence. Faulkner's growth as a novelist was thus most unusual, for he evolved as a writer of fiction not from short stories to novels as most novelists do, but rather from short poems to poem sequences (novels in poetry à la Conrad Aiken and other early Modernists) to novels. Until recently, however, Faulkner's sequences have received scant

---

10. See Appendix A for list of known versions of each poem.

11. Keen Butterworth, "A Census of Manuscripts and Typescripts of William Faulkner's Poetry," *Mississippi Quarterly* 26 (Summer 1973): 333–359, and reprinted with addenda in James B. Meriwether, ed., *A Faulkner Miscellany* (Jackson: University Press of Mississippi, 1974), pp. 70–97. I use his census as a basis for my list of versions of poems in *Vision in Spring* in Appendix A.

12. As late as the 1940s and 1950s Faulkner was still making up verse. Some of it was even funny. According to Jill Faulkner Summers, beginning when she was four or five "he told me stories in verse at night about this squirrel named Virgil Jones who had wild adventures. The end of the refrain running through it was 'And out stepped Virgil Jones with his guitar.' I loved it. He was the Scaramouche of the animal world—very rakish with a luxuriant plume of a tail. He was always in trouble and always victorious. He always came out on top though seldom justifiably. I know my mother was—or perhaps she pretended to be—horrified. She thought the stories were funny but she'd remonstrate with him about them—she thought they should have *some* sort of moral. He continued the saga for my son Tad and even made a record, which is lost, as is the book [of Virgil Jones] he made for me" (Jill Faulkner Summers, interviews, 23 October 1979 and 29 July 1980).

13. Cleanth Brooks, *William Faulkner, towards Yoknapatawpha and Beyond* (New Haven: Yale University Press, 1978), pp. ix, xi.

critical attention. In consequence, our understanding of his maturation as an artist has been obscured. This aspect of Faulkner's poetry—one that suggests that from the first Faulkner's intentions leaned toward sustained and experimental forms of narrative—is apparent in all the cycles.

Vision in Spring, though flawed, is a fascinating work, for it marks a turning point in Faulkner's long self-education. As he wrote *Vision in Spring*, and perhaps even more as he revised it (during those apparently fallow years of 1922 to 1923) to create *Orpheus*, he learned at last to separate himself from his dream and so to find his true voice. To be a poet was a dream he had tried to realize from the time (about 1916) that he began to write in earnest, a dream, expressed first in *The Marble Faun*, "for things I know yet cannot know." As stated by the Marble Faun, Faulkner's earliest *pierrotique* mask, to be a poet was an impossible ideal. For, if attained, this ideal conferred divinity: "They sorrow not that they are dumb: / For they would not a god become" (*TMF* XVII, p. 48). Faulkner reiterates this ideal throughout his apprenticeship to poetry and does not begin to reject it until he writes *Vision in Spring*, the cycle that signals and describes his transformation from mediocre poet and dreamer to potentially brilliant novelist.

Because *Vision in Spring* is apprenticeship writing, its interest attaches more to the process than the product of composition—to the young artist developing formal structures, techniques, and thematic concerns that, in his novels, will support what Helen Vendler calls "new forms for consciousness."[14] Faulkner's lifelong concern with poetry, coupled with his abandoned desire to be a poet, shapes the form, the language, and the moral preoccupations of his major novels.

Faulkner's use of the poem sequence as a formal structure and his adoption of the Pierrot mask (both developed most completely in *Vision in Spring*) are of special significance in any analysis of the relation of Faulkner's poetry to his fiction. Pierrot's character, even when disguised, informs and animates the protagonists of much of Faulkner's poetry. In the first sequence he began to write (a cycle of pastoral eclogues) Faulkner calls his *pierrotique* protagonist the Marble Faun. In *The Lilacs*, this figure appears variously as an airman in pursuit of a nympholeptic vision ("a white woman, a white wanton"); as an adolescent boy held in the "snare" by the commanding "caress" of a Miss Havisham–like woman; and as a young man lamenting the loss of a love never actually possessed, the heart of "a dead dancer." In *Vision in Spring*, where Faulkner ascertains the severe limitations of his mask, Pierrot becomes most like some of Faulkner's fictional protagonists.

When he turned to fiction, Faulkner discarded this mask only to reinvent Pierrot-like figures for the cast of Yoknapatawpha. Experimenting with Pierrot's many voices in the formal contexts of his poem sequences, but especially in *Vision in Spring*, taught Faulkner ways to cast off the mask while retaining in his writing those

14. Helen Vendler, "A Talk with Helen Vendler," *Chicago Literary Review* 5 (June 1981).

qualities that made it so imaginatively compelling. When he gave up his *pierrotique* mask, Faulkner did not abandon either its language—the language of dream—or its character. Rather, he began to make these dreams more intelligible. The protean poet-dreamer resurfaces in his tragic and comic fictional protagonists.

While Pierrot provided Faulkner with a basic character type possessed of multiple and often contradictory voices, the poem sequence offered a formal structure in which he could explore multilinear, noncausal, episodic, narrative modes of presentation. Sequences, particularly *Vision in Spring,* proved extremely effective forms within which to split, multiply, and then counterpoint Pierrot's voices through an increasingly complicated and sophisticated style. Thus, as a poet, Faulkner was experimenting with stylistic devices and thematic arrangements that closely relate to the kind of organization we associate with his and other, more elliptical Modernist novels. Such novels are condensed, like much lyric poetry, in the sense that the reader must supply narrative connections. They also are highly organized. Different as they are in other respects, Joyce's *Ulysses,* Virginia Woolf's *Mrs. Dalloway,* and Faulkner's *The Sound and the Fury* supply paradigms of this kind of ellipsis and condensation. For Faulkner, verse was not a dead end; rather, it was a valuable and enduring beginning: through it he advanced toward "authentic and fluent speech."

QUESTIONS OF INFLUENCE

In *Vision in Spring* one can also trace Faulkner's daring, artistic response to a confluence of intellectual and emotional events, as embodied in its ambivalent and ambiguous love poetry. The role *Vision in Spring* plays in the evolution of Faulkner's creative imagination demands that we attend to the voices Faulkner fails at or succeeds in subsuming as he writes the book that will begin to free him from the poet's mask he has worn since 1916, when he penned his earliest Swinburnian lyrics. If we ignore, in Harold Bloom's terms, the strong precursors Faulkner wrestles with here "even to the death" of his poetic voice, we will miss a most important event. *Vision in Spring* reveals Faulkner in the process of "clearing imaginative space" for himself so he may "appropriate" his own voice.[15] Faulkner the successful fiction writer could loudly proclaim his "failure" as a poet because he knew that in that failure lay his triumph as a novelist.

Vision in Spring stands in his apprenticeship as a record of Faulkner's intellectual journey from the nineteenth-century world of Keats, Swinburne, Tennyson, and the Symbolists through the early twentieth-century world of the Modernists. While he derived essential impetus for the imaginative leaps of *Vision in Spring* from dialogue with and imitation of many poets, Conrad Aiken, from whom Faulkner bor-

15. Harold Bloom, *The Anxiety of Influence, a Theory of Poetry* (Oxford: Oxford University Press, 1973).

rowed poetic techniques, particularly Aiken's conception of a "symphonic" poem sequence, proved especially valuable. He also assimilated Freudian theories of perception in part through Aiken's poems.[16] *Vision in Spring* shows Faulkner attempting Modernist techniques in an extended piece of work a full four years before he wrote his first novel. Its form and content anticipate the shape and style of *Soldiers' Pay, The Sound and the Fury, Light in August,* and other fiction. Evidence that accumulates from analysis of this and earlier cycles casts new light on such old questions as whether *Go Down Moses* is a mere collection of stories or a unified work, or whether *The Wild Palms* is two novellas or a novel. It also enriches the meaning of stories like "Black Music" and "Pantaloon in Black," and shows both *Soldiers' Pay* and *Mosquitoes* to be more interesting and complex than previously thought.

What was the nature of Faulkner's dialogue with Aiken, a dialogue that comes to include T. S. Eliot as, in *Vision*'s climactic poem, Faulkner parodies "The Love Song of J. Alfred Prufrock"? Since this parody is directed at his own as well as Eliot's and Aiken's Pierrot masks, it serves to free Faulkner momentarily from the limited register of his Pierrot voices. Thus, *Vision* closes with what can be recognized as a typical conclusion of a Faulkner novel although in a highly condensed form, containing specific formal, thematic, and metaphoric elements also present in the endings of *Flags in the Dust* and *The Sound and the Fury.*

MAJOR THEMES

The dominant themes in *Vision in Spring,* though familiar, are important. Like the Faun of *The Marble Faun* and Pierrot and Marietta of *The Marionettes, Vision*'s protean narrator Pierrot asks,

> Who am I, . . . who am I
> To stretch my soul out rigid across the sky?
> Who am I to chip the silence with footsteps,
> Then see the silence fill my steps again? (*VIS* III, pp. 25–26)

Pierrot's quest for identity and other themes are repeated with variations throughout the sequence's major movements. As Aiken claimed to in his sequences, Faulkner attempts to manipulate words as a composer would musical phrases. Thus variations on important images, words, and phrases are repeated throughout the work. Aiken's symphonies also suggested new ways of handling narrative voice and multiple points of view. Faulkner found in Aiken's work, as he had in other poets', compatible poetic themes. In *Vision in Spring,* as in Aiken's sequences, nympholepsy, the plight of the actor-poet, and the mnemonic character of music figure prominently. Symbols of the quest for self through nympholeptic visions (shadows, mirrors, immersions into

16. For a discussion of the Faulkner/Aiken/Freud connection, see Sensibar, *Origins*, chap. 7.

dreamscapes through water and music), the sense of loneliness and impotence, and accounts of unfulfilled, thwarted, or unfulfillable desire permeate Faulkner's *Vision*. Place, as in Aiken's symphonic poems, is intentionally vague and dreamlike. Like Aiken's fictional world, it is sometimes a barren and silhouetted cityscape, becoming at other times an unparticularized, surreal pastoral or seascape. Faulkner, like Aiken, uses place as a metaphor for elaborating Pierrot's feelings and perceptions. These, reflected in and filtered through Pierrot's inner voices—what Aiken called "the image-stream in the mind which we call consciousness—these hold the stage." The multiple narrators of Faulkner's earlier sequence *The Lilacs* have been replaced by what appears to be a single but multifaceted voice similar to that of an Aiken "symphony." Occasionally, as in Aiken's sequences, an impersonal narrator intrudes upon the "I" to question or lecture.

FAULKNER'S *PIERROTIQUE* MASK

Who is this "I" of *Vision*? He calls himself Pierrot, and in certain moods, particularly in parts of the third poem, "Nocturne," and the tenth, "The Dancer," he sounds very much like Pierrot of *The Marionettes*. But in this sequence Faulkner has added a broader range of modulations to his voice and a contemporary echo to the metaphors of Pierrot's interior imaginings. Here the Symbolist mask of the would-be poet, repeating phrases spoken previously by Faulkner's earlier narrators, alternates with a Pierrot of a distinctly Modernist cast. Faulkner's new Pierrot is related to the *pierrotique* personas of the poems Eliot wrote between 1904 and 1911 "under the sign of Laforgue" and to the narrators of Aiken's poems written between 1911 and 1920.[17] He muses on many of the same subjects and expresses himself in similar metaphors. In terms of superficial borrowing, many of his lines are simply variants of lines from Aiken's or Eliot's earlier poems.

Faulkner chose Pierrot, the paradigm Symbolist poet-*isolé*, in part because he was in the air. Aside from Aiken, Eliot, and Wallace Stevens, numerous poets were turning out Pierrot poems. They proliferated in poetry publications as diverse as those

---

17. Storey quoting T. S. Eliot on himself in *Pierrot: A Critical History*, p. 160. Faulkner steals phrases from these poems—"Conversation Galante," "Portrait of a Lady," and "The Love Song of J. Alfred Prufrock"—to ornament *The Marble Faun*, *The Lilacs*, and *Vision in Spring*. Faulkner parodies "Prufrock" in the climactic poem in *Vision*. Faulkner's subject in his poetry is the quintessential masker himself, Pierrot, the darling of the Symbolists and early Modernists. This nineteenth-century Pierrot's "vacillations between two dramatic and psychological 'types'"—the amoral Harlequin of the old Italian comedy and Hamlet—explain both the great attraction and the severe limitation of his appeal as a poetic persona (see Storey, *Pierrot: A Critical History*, p. xiv). Faulkner's parody of both Prufrock and his own Pierrot in *VIS* IX shows that he had become aware of Pierrot's limitations. For a full discussion of Conrad Aiken's early *pierrotique* narrators, see Frederick Hoffman, *Conrad Aiken* (New York: Twayne Publishers, 1962).

of Harriet Monroe and W. S. Braithwaite.[18] But Faulkner also chose Pierrot because he was maneuvering toward a persona who would bring together and subsume diverse sources and problems. Finally, he chose Pierrot for personal reasons. Pierrot's paralyzing duality of vision, his doubleness, was something Faulkner recognized. It sprang from a dilemma almost eerily familiar. Pierrot was Faulkner's fictional representation of his own fragmented state. In pretending simultaneously to be the wounded war hero, the great airman, the British dandy, the poet-aesthete, and the tramp, Faulkner too was playing forms of Pierrot. As writer and illustrator of his own books, Faulkner was attempting dual idealized roles: the artist (like his mother, Maud) and the poet-outcast.

Pierrot then becomes a perfect emblem for his private tension. As Faulkner presents him in *The Marionettes*, where half of him is constricted by drink to a world of inaction, impotence, and dreams, the character mirrors a solution Faulkner actually tried. Pierrot also suggests Faulkner's father, Murry, who drank to escape the disapproval of his wife and father. The other half, Pierrot's Shade, the Rake, is a fictionalized ideal, a fantastically successful poet and lover, who wields his poetry as a soldier does his sword: for conquest. For Faulkner's Pierrot, the enemy is most often, and paradoxically, his poetry's ideal woman, whose perfection makes her unattainable.

In *Vision*, Pierrot, his character enlarged, his voice range multiplied by Faulkner's reading of the Modernists and his conscious and sophisticated use of the sequence as a narrative poetic form, continues the quest he began in *The Marble Faun*. The more personal, colloquial voice Faulkner gives him in many of *Vision*'s poems permits him insights not granted his marble statue or the drink-numbed hero of Faulkner's Symbolist play.

Faulkner's fictional characters, particularly his major ones, exhibit many *pierrotique* elements. What *Vision* provides—most spectacularly in its third poem—is the essence of what will become his fictional Pierrots. When Pierrot of *Vision in Spring* is viewed in the dual context of the writer's later life and work, reasons for the hold he continued to exert on Faulkner's imagination are clarified. Donald Mahon in *Soldiers' Pay* is a good fictional analogue: like Pierrot he has tried to fly—to accomplish the impossible—and, like him, he has been punished, paralyzed by wounds to head, hands, and eyes. He will never create anything or control his actions (compare passages from *SP*, p. 294, to *VIS*, pp. 12, 13, 16, 47–54).[19]

Despite these and other similarities that identify Faulkner as the author of both works, an immense imaginative gap separates Donald Mahon from Pierrot. Donald is believable. Pierrot is not. The reason has a lot to do with voice. Donald, a *pierrotique* figure, is not, as was Pierrot, Faulkner's mask. This *pierrotique* mask dis-

18. In January 1921 Phil Stone gave Faulkner William Stanley Braithwaite's *Anthology of Magazine Verse for 1920* (Blotner, *Faulkner*, p. 299).

19. For a full discussion of this comparison, see Sensibar, *Origins*, chap. 9. William Faulkner, *Soldiers' Pay* (New York: Horace Liveright, pbk., 1970).

carded, Faulkner no longer seems inhibited by a fictional voice he can easily identify as his own. With appropriate distance put between himself and his fictional characters he can begin to explore the implications of this early but still powerful private fantasy.

Turning to Faulkner's later life, we see this fantasy continuing to figure largely in his imagination, where it appeared as a nightmare vision of failure. In this nightmare Faulkner transformed himself into a combination of the tortured Pierrot and his well-known wounded pilot pose. Meta Doherty Wilde reports Faulkner's hallucination in the midst of a drinking bout:

> . . . I saw Bill *huddled on one corner of the bed, hands stretched out, palms foremost, as if to ward off something menacing. His head was bent, eyes* mercifully turned away from whatever it was that threatened him, and he moved as I observed him into a *crouched position—knees up, shoulders sagging* . . .
>
> He looked up, no recognition whatever in his face, and screamed, "They're going to get me! Oh, Lordy, oh, Jesus!" He covered his head with hands that alternately flailed and supplicated, shouting over and over in a litany of dread, "They're coming down at me! Help me! Don't let them! They're coming at me! No! No!"
>
> . . . when I tried to touch him, he recoiled from me convulsively.
>
> "Who?" I asked him. "Who's trying to hurt you?"
>
> "They're diving down at me. Swooping. Oh, Lordy!"
>
> "Faulkner, what are you talking about? Who's after you?"
>
> He turned a face as white as library paste toward me. "The Jerries! Can't you see them?" Suddenly *he was doubled over, trying to crawl into himself. "Here they come again! They're after me! They're trying to shoot me out of the sky. . . . they're out to kill me."* (Emphasis added)[20]

Wilde never read *Vision in Spring*. Even if she had, the remarkable parallels between her description of Faulkner here and Faulkner's description of Pierrot in "Nocturne" would still be uncanny. This incident adds credence to the hypothesis that Pierrot was, throughout Faulkner's career, his nemesis. When he could take this nemesis out of the realm of private dream and fantasy and transform him into a fictional figure of either comic or tragic stature, he gained momentary mastery over him. Otherwise Pierrot remained for Faulkner—especially when he drank—a figure of dread and fear, the embodiment of failure in art and life, his other self, the dark double who in fiction he so triumphantly re-created.

Pierrot is the moral center of *Vision in Spring*. When we read this and earlier sequences in conjunction with the novels, we can trace Pierrot's transformations and understand why he remains in Faulkner's fiction, directing Faulkner's intentions

20. Meta Carpenter Wilde, *A Loving Gentleman* (New York: Simon and Schuster, 1976), p. 143. For a complete listing of other Faulkner pilot stories, see Brooks, *Yoknapatawpha and Beyond*, pp. 403–406; also his remarks on Faulkner's novel *Pylon* (1935), pp. 395–406.

throughout his career. In his fictional guises Pierrot always represents specific forms of moral failure or weakness: failure to love, failure to create, failure to grow, and failure to choose. Pierrot has spoken in previous poems, but fragmenting his voices, as Faulkner did in *Vision*, was a necessary first step in mastering him. To parody him, even if only briefly, was the second. To introduce an impersonal but not necessarily reliable narrator was the third.

Faulkner's subsequent fictional treatments of Pierrot are prefigured in *Vision*. He reappears not only as aspects of Januarius Jones, Donald Mahon, and Margaret Powers in *Soldiers' Pay* but also as parts of Quentin Compson in *The Sound and the Fury*, Gail Hightower and Joe Christmas in *Light in August*, Horace Benbow in *Sanctuary*, and Miss Rosa Coldfield and Sutpen in *Absalom, Absalom!* But we can only know this and comprehend its meaning in terms of Faulkner's intention if we know from reading his poetry, especially the three sequences of 1919 to 1921 that culminate with *Vision in Spring*, how to recognize and weigh the import of the *pierrotique* elements in those and other Faulkner characters.

THE FORMAL DESIGN

Vision in Spring is difficult to read, in part because what Arthur F. Kinney and others have called the "reconstitutive" quality of Faulkner's style is not yet fully functional; it is difficult to attend to because the depression of its persona, Pierrot, can easily cast a soporific pall. But close reading is worth the effort for the rich information it yields about the genesis of Faulkner's style and the moral and intellectual preoccupations that direct it.

Unlike *The Lilacs* or *The Marble Faun*, *Vision in Spring* carries in its title an abstract noun: vision. The singular suggests that the sequence derives from the "vision" of a central consciousness and that the series of poems reflects and counterpoints different aspects of "vision in spring." All the voices heard in Faulkner's poem (the third-person impersonal narrator excepted) arise from one dramatic center. The book's title also places it in time. Unlike *The Marble Faun*'s, *Vision*'s central intelligence experiences no diurnal progression. His body inhabits a wavering, indistinct present while his mind dwells in an emphatically vivid past. By claiming as his own the title of one of Swinburne's best lyrics, "A Vision of Spring in Winter," Faulkner suggests that this sequence, like *The Marble Faun*, is in some way a dialogue with or comment upon the echoed writer's poetic vision. Faulkner significantly leaves out the final words of Swinburne's title and changes the preposition. His is not a vision *of* spring that throws attention on the object, but a vision *in* spring that keeps attention on the subject. He does not need the last phrase, for the "winter" of *Vision*'s persona (like that of the Marble Faun) lies within. Faulkner's title has, as well, internal reference. It recalls the vision poems in *The Lilacs* sequence and the Marble Faun's limited vision, suggesting that this new sequence may be a kind of thematic progression from these earlier sequences.

With vision established as the general subject, Faulkner uses the table of contents to suggest what kinds of vision concern his persona and to indicate that his visions are both related and ordered. Faulkner numbered each poem sequentially and titled all but four. The titles hint at one of *Vision*'s themes: the intimate relationship between vision and artistic creativity. The timeless arts—poetry and philosophy, dance, music, painting—appear in all titles but the first and last, where time, always the frame of art, is asserted. The titles function like program music titles, indicating the extramusical idea Faulkner will develop within the narrative form of what Aiken called the "verbal symphonic poem." Words take the place of musical notation as they are integrated into "verbal melodies." The narrator of Faulkner's verbal symphonic poem contains within his consciousness the symphony's themes. The narrator's consciousness is thus the symphony's center or focus, and the theme or themes that dominate his consciousness become the "verbal symphony's" themes. How the themes are played against and upon each other becomes the dramatic action of the poem.

In *Vision in Spring*, minor themes are subordinated to give metaphoric and tonal texture to the larger issue: whether vision is an acceptable substitute for more traditional forms of masculine action.[21] If it is, does it apply to *all* kinds of vision or only certain kinds? Finally, how does a writer, an artist, determine which kinds of vision are acceptable and which must be discouraged or ignored? Resolution of this last issue implies the making of important aesthetic and moral choices, and in *Vision in Spring* Faulkner finds his way to a partial resolution. The voices in *Vision in Spring* are working toward definitions of true and false vision. But because, as he writes this sequence, Faulkner himself is not clear as to what constitutes true vision, the definitions and answers the voices suggest seem confusing and even contradictory.

POINT OF VIEW: PIERROT'S VISION AS CONTROLLING METAPHOR

In *Vision in Spring*, vision is a metaphorical not a literal act; vision refers to what the inner eye or the imagination sees. With this kind of vision as the chief mode of perception, the dominant narrative structural devices shift from calendar to conceptual time and from narrative description of external events to the associative aspects of the persona's interior musings. While calendar time frames the sequence (Faulkner titles the opening and closing poems "Vision in Spring" and "April"), time is static. Faulkner's emphasis is upon conceptual or interior chronology: what Aiken called "the image stream in the mind" of Pierrot.

Contrasted to what Pierrot's voices hear as actual but deceptive music is his own memory or impression of music, "soundless rings" or "quiet sound" or a "silence [that] sings" (pp. 37, 36). This kind of music, emanating from his own imagination,

21. Frank Kermode, *The Romantic Image* (New York: Vintage, 1957), pp. 23–29.

can lead to vision capable of creating a compelling work of art. Pierrot does not reject this vision outright, but seems, nonetheless, to fear it. Thus Faulkner again reaffirms and reinstates his voices after briefly parodying them (*VIS* IX, pp. 55–64). How Faulkner manipulates vision in this sequence provides a map of his progress toward understanding the forms his own imagination must embrace in order for him to consider his act of translating poetic vision an adequate moral substitute for a life of physical action. While writing as poet, Faulkner attempts to live the active life through his pose as an RAF officer. Jill Summers' description of her father's attitude toward war illustrates his continuing ambivalence: "He really did regret not being in action. He loved battles and would often quote Henry V, 'Take me, take a soldier, take a king.' He said all men felt about war the same way, that boys had toy guns to play with while men had war. But he didn't like modern-day war—killing. He liked the panoply. That's why he liked the RAF."[22] As he writes this sequence Faulkner is learning to differentiate between active and passive or fruitful and unfruitful kinds of vision.

Even in 1921 Faulkner was less dependent than Aiken on traditional narrative devices. Thus he did not, like Aiken, indicate breaks in his larger "more narrative movements" either in his table of contents or in his text. However, as in Aiken's symphonies, a four-part structure, unified by a recurring theme, is discernible. *Vision*'s central intelligence, residing in Pierrot's multiple voices, repeats, varies, and reinterprets key melodies played, seen, heard, remembered, and imagined by him and an impersonal narrator. These melodies take the forms of monologues, soliloquies, and occasional interior and exterior dialogues, which, as they transform image to concept, create *Vision*'s structure and determine its style.

Of *Vision*'s four sections, three are of almost equal length, with the fourth distinctly shorter. Having introduced his themes in *Vision*'s first movement, Faulkner uses the others to develop and counterpoint the themes through Pierrot's multiple voices and visions. Pierrot's visions are occasionally interrupted by an impersonal third-person narrator. In the first poem he introduces Pierrot: "And at last, having followed a voice that cried within him . . . he stood, aghast" (p. 1). But not until the fourth movement does he assert an identifiable and separate point of view as he replaces Pierrot and appears to direct the final vision to its problematic resolution.

Vision's opening movement (poems I–III, pp. 1–29) invokes the first of Pierrot's dreamworlds, a nonspecific setting in which Pierrot, in the role of poet-*isolé*, introduces some of the major themes Faulkner will develop within its "polyphonic musical structure." Faulkner's experiment in "abstract three dimensional verse" begins with music.[23] Bell tones lead to Pierrot's first vision: "A sudden vagueness of

22. Jill Faulkner Summers, interview, 16 March 1982.

23. See Faulkner's thoughtful and serious review of Conrad Aiken's *Turns and Movies* reprinted in Carvel Collins, ed., *Early Prose and Poetry of William Faulkner* (London: Jonathan Cape, 1963), pp. 74–77. Faulkner's language here demonstrates familiarity with Aiken's criticism and his poetry.

pain," which he claims is "my heart . . . that broke" (p. 1). He mourns the passing of time and the failure of his quests for love, fame, and a knowledge of his own identity: "Who am I . . . ?" (*VIS* III, p. 25). In the next pages Pierrot, occasionally helped by the impersonal narrator, delineates some facets of his own character and emerges from the third and longest poem of the movement, "Nocturne," as a composite of the Marble Faun, the two Pierrots of *The Marionettes*, and the voice(s) of *The Lilacs*. Like them, he appears to be a depressed, fragmented, will-less figure who lives primarily in a dreamlike world of nympholeptic fantasies. This frozen boy/man "spins and whirls," caged in his stark, moonlit world of icy peaks and deserts. As he spins, "His bloodless hands are like two candle flames . . . / Beside the corpse of his face laid on his breast" (p. 11). To ensure that his readers will connect this deathlike Pierrot to the unnamed voice in *Vision*'s first two poems, Faulkner reintroduces phrases used earlier.

A scene shift in the second movement (poems IV–VIII, pp. 30–54) is signaled by its first poem's title, "After the Concert." Another voice describes how music is reexperienced "after the concert" and what visions attend this memory. Replacing the first movement's amorphous dreamscape is an impressionistic but contemporary townlike landscape: a world of concerts, movies, lamplit streets. The voice of Faulkner's Modernist Pierrot informs much of *Vision*'s second movement; it imitates and echoes Aiken's *pierrotique* narrators, recalling the poetic persona heard briefly in *The Lilacs*. But this Pierrot sounds less forlorn: more sociable and active, he speaks occasionally of "us" and "we" in contrast to the earlier Pierrot's solitary "I." He plays a sophisticated, slightly world-weary lover addressing a much younger, very naïve (read unthreatening), childlike woman:

> You are so young. And frankly you believe
> This world, this darkened street, this shadowed wall
> Are bright with beauty you passionately know
> Cannot fade nor cool nor die at all.
> (*VIS* V, p. 34)

In the eighth and closing poem of this second section, the Pierrot of the first movement returns. The music of false vision—"bells on golden wings"—reintroduces the first movement's major theme: the dangers of false vision's seductive music, bells that confine Pierrot to a living death as they "echo his life away" (*VIS* VIII, p. 47).

The third and climactic movement (poems IX–XII, pp. 55–82) begins with the important "Love Song" (*VIS* IX), in which Pierrot parodies the *pierrotique* voices of the two prior movements. The parodist asserts that "dream is death"—dream that reflects or mirrors but does not illuminate and give new meaning to old visions (*VIS*, p. 60). Self-parody is an indicator of self-knowledge. Vision that leads to self-knowledge, which calls upon memory not merely to relive the past but to give the past new meaning, is true vision. The moment of self-parody is brief; Pierrot's old voices reassert themselves in the poems that follow. Nonetheless, his voices will not control the sequence's closing statement. First in the guise of Pierrot the poet-*isolé* (poem X), then as a Modernist *pierrotique* figure (poem XI), and finally as the poet-musician Orpheus (poem XII), the combined Pierrot voices reassert that questing after love is dangerous, depressing, and disappointing. As the third movement concludes, all the *pierrotique* voices, the parodist excepted, are opting for a vision of a silent, frigid, isolated world where, as passive voyeurs, they can freely dream about the past: a womblike Aikenesque "sea in which I sink, yet cannot drown" (*VIS*, p. 81). The movement's concluding voice, Orpheus/Pierrot, like the other voices has lost his ideal woman. As in the first two movements, Pierrot stands alone; but rather than simply daydreaming, he now *sings* about his lost love. Endowed with Orpheus's stature and the godlike creative powers the Marble Faun wished for, he claims to know the answer to the question Pierrot posed in *Vision*'s first movement. He knows who he is. Orpheus then defines himself in seven different ways in nine short strophes. But his definitions are overblown and no more satisfactory than Pierrot's earlier nonanswers in "Nocturne" (*VIS* III, pp. 26, 27).[24]

An abrupt scenic and tonal shift occurs in *Vision*'s fourth and final movement (poems XIII–XIV, pp. 83–88), where Faulkner banishes all Pierrot's voices. The impersonal narrator replacing him states that Pierrot's visions are dead: the "lidless blaze" of the noonday sun has burned away Pierrot's Swinburnian dreams of "shortening-breasted nymphs" (*VIS*, p. 83). The graveyard where Pierrot's false visions lie buried—real death—replaces the imagined death scenes of his previous visions. Setting and descriptive language anticipate the setting and metaphorical landscape in the concluding chapters of *Flags in the Dust*, Faulkner's first Yoknapatawpha novel. Faulkner's method of distancing the reader from his personas' dreamworlds anticipates, in a condensed and simplified form, the method he later uses to show Miss Jenny separating herself from her beloved but suicidal nephew, a *pierrotique* figure from *Flags*. In "April," *Vision*'s concluding poem, the impersonal narrator appears to be returning to the sequence's beginning. Faulkner has retained many of the nature metaphors from *Vision*'s first movement, but by giving vision over to the consciousness of his impersonal narrator, he can modulate the tone. The time is still spring but Faulkner's vision is new. For the first time in his poetry, the past is given new meaning, a meaning supplied not by Pierrot or by the narrator but by us as we listen to Faulkner's polyphony and draw upon the voices' combined effect to reach our own conclusions.

FROM ART TO LIFE: *VISION IN SPRING* AS A LOVE POEM

> I don't know whether . . . any writer could say just how he identifies himself with his characters. Quite often the young man will write about himself simply

24. See Sensibar, *Origins*, chap. 10.

> because himself is what he knows best. That he is using himself as the standard of measure, and to simplify things, he writes about himself as—perhaps as he presumes himself to be, maybe he hopes himself to be, or maybe as he hates himself for being.[25]

In the equivocal yet truthful mode we associate with him, William Faulkner here comments on the wide range of autobiographical motivation operating in young writers and present in their work. Such writing has been characterized as, in general, the most transparently autobiographical.[26] The growth of an artist's mind is not a purely intellectual affair. Faulkner's reading of Modernists and his growing facility with poetic technique cannot account completely for either the delicacy or the painful clarity of some of his insights in *Vision*. According to Blotner, Faulkner made this booklet for Estelle Oldham Franklin and gave it to her when she returned to Oxford during the summer of 1921 for her annual visit. She had brought her two-and-a-half-year-old daughter, Victoria ("Cho-Cho"), but, as usual, had left her husband, Cornell, in Hawaii. The visit marked Estelle's third extended stay in Oxford since her marriage in April 1918.[27] That Faulkner gave *Vision* to her is significant because knowing that he chose to continue their relationship, despite or perhaps because of her marriage, is essential to understanding the preoccupations of *Vision in Spring*. Not only was Estelle still married to another man and thus safely unattainable, she was also mostly absent. Both facts made her an ideal recipient of and muse for the love poems Faulkner wrote in *Vision*.

Love, or rather its absence, is the subject of much of Faulkner's poetry. Like his earlier sequences, *Vision in Spring* provides a continuing record of the poet's thinly disguised attempts to come to terms with his own sexuality, together with his ambivalence, already alluded to, about the conflicting roles of artist and man of action. Not surprisingly, the people most closely associated with Faulkner's life as a poet, a life he preserved for certain occasions, are the women he loved. Besides retaining its position as a touchstone for certain kinds of emblematic scenes and metaphorical structures in his novels, verse played a special role in Faulkner's private life: he continued throughout his career to write, recite, and read poetry to these women. Among those we know of are his mother, his Great-Aunt Bama McLean, his wife, Estelle, his daughter, Jill, and Helen Baird, Meta Doherty Wilde, and Joan Williams.

In discussing Joan Williams' relation to Faulkner, David Minter observes that in his letters to her he uses language—culled from Rostand's *Cyrano*—that he had

---

25. William Faulkner, 25 February 1957, in Frederick L. Gwynn and Joseph Blotner, eds., *Faulkner in the University* (New York: Random House, 1959), p. 25.
26. Walter Jackson Bate, *John Keats* (Cambridge, Mass.: Harvard University Press, 1963), *The Burden of the Past and the English Poet* (New York: Norton, 1970, 1972), and *Samuel Johnson* (New York: Harcourt Brace Jovanovich, 1977).
27. According to Blotner, Estelle's first visit home after her marriage to Franklin and move to Honolulu occurred June 1919 to 29 September 1919. Her baby daughter was then four months old. Estelle's second visit occurred in May 1920 and her third in May 1921.

used first in love declarations to Helen Baird.[28] Actually this doubling and repetition had begun much earlier. Two examples of it are the similarity in phrasing between Faulkner's dedicatory words to Cho-Cho (but really to Estelle) in the copy he gave her of *The Marionettes*: ". . . this, a shadowy fumbling in windy darkness," and his inscription to Helen in *Mayday*: "to thee O wise and lovely this: a fumbling in darkness."[29] The day before he bound *Mayday* for his concurrent unavailable love interest, Helen Baird, Faulkner rebound *Vision in Spring* for Estelle. Faulkner's love letters in the early 1950s to Meta Doherty Wilde and Joan Williams, often echoing each other, are sometimes written only days apart.[30] This suggests that Faulkner thought of and experienced the women he loved in an undifferentiated way. What was important from the beginning, and remained so, was not the woman herself but Faulkner's imaginary re-creation of her in language. He expresses this attitude most clearly in his love poems in *Vision in Spring*, especially in the untitled sixth poem, "Marriage," and "The Dancer," where what affects and is valued by the would-be poet is not the woman herself but his imaginary vision of her, which he does not wish disturbed by her language or movement (see *VIS*, pp. 38–39, 65–66, 70, 74).

During the summer of 1921, Faulkner continued, as he had since he returned from the RAF in December 1918, to live at home with his parents. But he gave *Vision in Spring*, a sequence brimming with musical allusions and unfulfilled desires, to a married woman who was a musician. Since, like his mother, Faulkner disliked, or claimed to dislike, actual music so much, it seems odd that ultimately he chose both a wife and a lover (Wilde) who were accomplished musicians.[31] It seems equally odd that he should in 1921 write a poetic sequence modeled on Aiken's verbal symphonies and containing poems with musical titles whose subjects are music, musicians, and dancers. (Faulkner was not fond of dancing either, preferring to watch, despite the fact that Estelle loved to dance.) Furthermore, Estelle was a person for whom his mother had little affection. Jill Faulkner Summers describes these women's relationship:

> Granny was not happy with any of her sons' marriages. There weren't a lot of people she liked besides her grandchildren. She disliked women in general, as a breed I think. She was an extremely down-to-earth, pragmatic little lady and I

28. David Minter, *William Faulkner, His Life and Work* (Baltimore: Johns Hopkins University Press, 1980), p. 231.
29. Noel Polk, ed., *The Marionettes* (Charlottesville: University of Virginia Press, 1977), p. 89. In his 1921 review of Aiken's *Turns and Movies* Faulkner characterized bad poets as "so many puppets fumbling in windy darkness." See Faulkner's review reprinted in Collins, *Early Prose and Poetry*, p. 75.
30. See Blotner, *Selected Letters*, pp. 297–362; Minter's valuable reconstruction in *His Life and Work*, chaps. 9, 10 (especially notes); and Wilde, *A Loving Gentleman*, pp. 316–328, plus her unpublished letters at the Humanities Research Center, University of Texas at Austin.
31. Sensibar, *Origins*, chap. 12.

> think she thought my mother was flighty—a sort of butterfly. There was very little interaction between Granny and my mother. Granny always wished that Pappy had not married Mama.

Summers observed that, although they shared physical characteristics, her mother and Maud Faulkner appeared to have little in common. But together they supplied his antithetical but concomitant desires for what a woman should be:

> My grandmother was very small, less than five feet tall. She was very tough and independent. She had painted above her stove "DON'T COMPLAIN DON'T EXPLAIN" and she would not answer to anyone for anything she did. She was stubborn with a very quiet wit. Sometimes she would say something and it wasn't until two or three minutes later that you realized how funny it was, or that perhaps you'd been had.
>
> Now one of the qualities about my mother that my father claimed distressed him was her *lack* of independence. In part I think this was because, for him, she was the idealized female figure in his poetry, and he saw everything about her through a romantic haze. There were always these two kinds of women in his mind and he needed both. The fact that my mother was physically frail appealed to him. The times he was most caring was when she was not well. He didn't appear to like toughness in her and flatly refused to see the strengths she did have. My mother was very Southern in that she could make any man believe that he was superman. She was also very manipulative for she was, like most Southern women, taught to obey implicitly, "so far as he is wise and she is able."[32]

Faulkner dedicated and gave much of his poetry to women he cared for. In 1924 he dedicated his one commercially published sequence, *The Marble Faun*, to his mother. In 1925 and 1926 he gave *Mayday* and *Helen: A Courtship* to Helen Baird. In the late 1930s he wrote and recited poetry to Meta Wilde, and in the 1950s he gave Joan Williams his own copy of *A Green Bough* (1933) and what to him throughout remained a symbol of his love language, *Cyrano*'s golden bell.[33] All these women resembled each other in several ways: they were independent, they were not available to Faulkner as marriage partners, and their interests, Williams excepted, were in art forms other than language (Faulkner's mother was also a painter).

Possibly Faulkner chose musical forms and subjects for *Vision in Spring* to please Estelle, who loved music. It might also be argued that, like other Modernists, he was interested in working within the convention of borrowing musical language and musical analogies for writing poetry. But neither of these explanations addresses the issue of why the language and themes of this sequence permeate so many emblematic scenes in Faulkner's novels. Such continuous usage suggests that this se-

32. Jill Faulkner Summers, interview, 30 July 1980. See also Ben Wasson, *Count No 'Count: Flashbacks to Faulkner* (Jackson: University Press of Mississippi, 1983), p. 77.

33. Joan Williams, interview, 20 June 1983. Also see Joan Williams, *The Wintering* (New York: Harcourt Brace Jovanovich, 1971), p. 229.

quence served as a touchstone for his imagination, one that continued to inspire him throughout his career.

The subjects of *Vision in Spring*—sex, love, power, impotence, death, and the powers of the imagination—are universal. Faulkner had written of them in earlier sequences but always literarily and obliquely. In *Vision*, as the poet makes metaphorical parallels between false and true vision and real and "silent" music, he comes closer than he ever has to breaking through that "white, opaque, distant" language: other poets' music.[34] Dimly through this music—to borrow his metaphor—we hear an original author's voice. In *Vision*, particularly in the three poems of its third movement, we begin to hear some life in Faulkner's voices and a hint of genuine emotion. Our reading experience becomes enriched as we see vague outlines of a "story" forming in the intricate formal and thematic connections Faulkner has worked out in the poems in his sequence. What then is the nature of Faulkner's poetic touchstone? Of what is it composed that makes it so rich with invention? The kinds of metaphorical connections Faulkner worked out here between music and vision served as a means for expressing imaginatively a series of conflicts and issues that figured prominently in his real life and in his fantasy life.

In 1921, when he wrote *Vision in Spring*, his temporary solution to these conflicts was a compromise. In the sequence, real music performed by other artists who also happen to be women (Colombine the actress, the dancers, the musicians) suggests and signifies Pierrot's fear that he will fail as a poet, or artist of words. Meanwhile, the sequence itself—love poetry drawing on music for its metaphorical structure and formal organization and addressed to a woman who, unlike his mother, loves music—is, in itself, Faulkner's bid for independence from his mother's exclusive love and her values.

Writing "Love Song," a poem whose only music is the "cadence" of Pierrot's feet, allowed Faulkner to make a further bid for independence. There he simultaneously unmasked both Eliot, a recognized poet, and that fearer of women, eternal adolescent, and mother's boy, the would-be poet-actor Pierrot. Parody enabled Faulkner to be more explicit in stating the previously hidden import of his fantasy material. In "The Dancer" and "Marriage" Pierrot confronts a real woman with whom he actually converses. She is no longer the safe and silent dream image of earlier poems like "Portrait." Furthermore, Pierrot begins to express an overt interest in and desire for adult sexual experiences. He no longer dwells exclusively in the isolated world of memory and dreams.

As Pierrot confronts these real women, the symbolic meaning of real music and dance (art forms these women initiate to charm him) is revealed to be death or failure. When he denies women's power over his fantasy life (the dancer is nothing

34. Faulkner used these adjectives when telling Wilde what he disliked about music, adjectives used in his own poetry to describe false vision (see *Vision in Spring*, passim; Sensibar, *Origins*, chap. 12; and Wilde, *A Loving Gentleman*, pp. 140, 178).

compared to his imaginative impression of her and the piano player cannot banish his sexual fantasy of her), he makes an emotional compromise. (Faulkner's college friend and sometime-editor Ben Wasson tells a story about Estelle dating from this period that may have some bearing on the private meaning of this poem to Faulkner.)[35] This denial permits him to demonstrate his continuing primary attachment to his mother. Faulkner represents her in his poetry as the Marble Faun's and Pierrot's "moon mother." She always "snares" her young victim, making him impotent, even as he is simultaneously obsessed with and repelled by a desire to experience an adult love relationship. In Faulkner's novels such victims persist. Their actual mothers are either malevolent, ineffectual, or dead. Popeye and Joe Christmas are examples.

Although Faulkner often referred to himself as a "failed poet," poetry was an essential part of his love relationships. Since poetry was the mode in which he communicated least effectively, it seems paradoxical that he should use it for the language of intimacy. But perhaps this is precisely the point. For Faulkner, love was always "opaque": symbolic of failure or anticipated failure. Thus he reserved his "failed" voice for it. It is thus fitting that often he invoked Cyrano to do so. Cyrano too could only express his love when he was absent and pretending to be someone else.[36] Perhaps also he used poetry—the language he so clearly associated with a dream state—to anesthetize his feelings in a "romantic haze" of false music: other poets' sounds and rhythms. Poetry continued, for Faulkner, to remain the language of his most impossible dreams: "'Perhaps they were right in putting love into books,' he thought quietly. 'Perhaps it could not live anywhere else'" (Gail Hightower, *Light in August*). But because this dream language also embodied his earliest and most fundamental fantasies, and it was the language by which he had learned their meaning, he returned to it throughout his life for inspiration.

---

35. Wasson, *Count No 'Count*, pp. 77–81.
36. See Blotner, *Faulkner*, vol. II, pp. 1761–1762 and rev. ed., pp. 187, 570, 578. Summers further illuminates this issue with her comments on the importance *Cyrano de Bergerac* had for Faulkner: "I think he identified with Cyrano in that he liked the idea of not being physically held responsible for what he said. It's really like being at a masquerade: you're not expected to complete an action, you can just talk and not be responsible for your words like Cyrano with Roxane" (Jill Faulkner Summers, interview, 16 March 1982).

VISION IN SPRING.

by

W. Faulkner.

Manuscript Edition. 1921.

A NOTE ON THE TEXT

This edition follows the author's original spelling, capitalization, and punctuation. However, because this edition was transcribed from a photocopy of the original typescript, it was often difficult to determine whether punctuation was typewritten or handwritten. Although handwritten underlinings and markings are not included, all changes affecting meaning have been set in brackets. As noted in the introduction, these accidentals and substantive changes are almost certainly not William Faulkner's or his wife's. Also in brackets, and with a question mark, I have set some conjectural corrections where a word either is partly illegible or is probably an unintentional misspelling. For ease of comparison, Faulkner's original pagination has been preserved. For the reader's convenience, a line count has been added. However, lines continued from one page to another in the original are concluded here on the page the line started on. In Vision in Spring *X, "The Dancer," a word missing in the text has been supplied in brackets from another version of that poem.*

Has broken and fallen away.

For I, who sought so much, I disregarded
The pennies one should hoard if one would buy
Peace, a corner for weary feet to stray to ---
Above him, swiftly, slenderly,

The trees tossed silver arms in sleeves of green,
And lustrous limbs and boughs
Moved in a hush[`]ed measure to an ancient music.
And then once more the brows

Of dancers he had dreamed before him floated,
Calm, unsaddened, in a sea of evening air;---

Lips repeating the melody, sustaining the cooling sunset
In the autumned stillness of their hair.

Lightly they rose about him, quickening in magic[,]
And his own life, so lax within his eyes,
Stirred again: this beauty touched him, quiet, weary.
Soft hands of skies

Delicately swung the narrow moon above him
And shivered the tips of trees, until he heard
The kissing of leaves; then lo! the dream had vanished.
He raised his hand, and stirred

And would have cried aloud, but was dumb as were the branches
That tightened to a faint refrain
Clinging like gossamer about them, that softly snared him.
Then the bells again

Like falling leaves, rose mirrored up from silence;
And he, in silence, with his empty heart
Pondered: I had this thing I sought, that now has escaped me
When it was shattered apart.

For I, who toiled through corridors of harsh laughter,
Who sought for light in dark reserves of pain; --
What shall I do, who am old and weary and lonely,--

Too weary to alone set forth again?

Softly above his head clear waves of darkness
Came up and filled the trees
And stilled the rigid branches to restless coral.
He rose from stiffened knees.

Spring, blown white along the faint starred darkness,
Arose again about him, like a wall
Beneath which he stood and watched, growing colder and colder,
A star immaculately fall.

Interlude.

Once more a soft starred evening falls
Upon these empty streets and walls;
Once more the world sinks into dark, he said,
Watching calm gusts of stars swept overhead
Like candle flames across a coffin blown --
And leaves a flare of light to whisper ancient stone.

Restless branches gestured on the dark
Above him; roof peaks, narrow[,] black and stark
Like sharpened foreheads, streamed with star-bright hair.
Some day he, too, must die. The air
Swung with the swinging trees above him, shadows tossed,

Futilely gestured,[--]fell,[--]in dark were lost.

I will watch them through clear glass
Of star-white silence, wearily enter there;---
Shadow and silence and dusk and stars -- . . . . they pass
In the vagrant music of their hair
To dance a last dark saraband
On powdered porphyry and coral sand.

Slowly, solemnly, and turn
With lifted throats, and hair that floats
With scarce moved knees, and soft breasts bare.
Slow gigantic waters slowly burn
The unstirred air.
Solemnly the clear fantastic pipes repeat

Quietly the dancing feet
Tread a measure full and strange,
A motion mazed with change oh [on? (illegible)] hushèd change;
Solemnly the clear fantastic reed
Clearly repeats a dark and simple need
Of someone, something, some still unfound bliss
To bless in quiet pain, and kiss . . . .

Slowly, solemnly, and turn
Across the world's dumb darkly dreaming face.
Raise your pipes: the melodies repeat
The calm majestic maze of dewy feet;
Solemnly the clear fantastic pipes refrain
The movement, solemnly again
The simple melodies repeat.

Slowly, solemnly, and turn.
Raise your face, grown calm and sad; your eyes,
Raise your mouth that seeks and sighs
In simple need of some untasted bliss
To bless in quiet pain, and kiss . . .

The horned gates swing to, and clang.
Pale empty waves of darkness which once sang
With delicate voices, heave up like knees
And fall, remotely fall, shuddering down far seas . . . .

He walked along the phantomed street
And rang the hollow pavement with his feet.

The World and Pierrot.
A Nocturne.

I.

Here, where the sound of worlds sinks down the sea
Mountainously echoed, wave by wave,
Pierrot would stand beside a night like a column of blue and silver.
The column scintillates with orange and green,
The column is dusty with facets of worlds that he has seen,
The column is frozen with stars of white and blue.
And now the air icily splinters and glistens
Delicately with the impact of the moon.
The moon is a luminous bird against a window flown
And Pierrot is a moth on the dark, alone,

A moth whose wings, scorched with cold,
Curl at the edges like two boneless hands.

Pierrot spins and whirls . . . .
Pierrot tugs at the darkness bright with worlds;
His shadow swiftly runs on the ice before him.

He whirls, cloaked in the starry darkness,
His bloodless hands are like two candle flames
Steadily burning on the dark
Beside the corpse of his face laid on his breast.
The wasted moon silently combs his hair:
He is in a cage of moonlight
Closing about him: the moon is a spider on the sky,
Weaving her icy silver across his heart.

Pierrot spins and whirls . . . .
The dark sea on a dark cliff silverly hurls
And freezes like teeth laid on the throat of the sky.
Swiftly laughter, swiftly voices fly
Like birds of ice with silver wings.

II.

Colombine leans above the taper flame:
Colombine flings a rose.
She flings a severed hand at Pierrot's feet.

Behind, a perpindicular [perpendicular?] wall of stars,
Below, a gleam of snows.
Pierrot spins and whirls, Pierrot is fleet;
He whirls his hands like birds before the moon.

Pierrot spins and whirls . . . .
His eyes are filled with facets of many worlds
Of white and blue and green;
And he would hide his head, yet the keen blue darkness
Cuts his arms away from his face.

Listen! A violin
Freezes into a blade so bright and thin,
It pierces through his brain, into his heart,
And he is spitted by a pin of music on the dark.

Swift the wisps of motion blown across the moon,--
Colombine flings a paper rose.
Pierrot [f]lits like a white moth on the dark.

Black the tapers, sharp thier [their?] mouths in starlight,
The sky desert with icy rootless flowers gauntly glows.
They are stiffly frozen, white and stark.

III.

Pierrot has watched the sunset sink among stark trees,
And the dark grow strange
And dusty with stars and silence,
And die; yet never change:
He, alone, must die by growing old.
And he sees the thin crisp darkness bowled
In the sky immaculately raised above his head,
He sees it suddenly whirl with fiery cold
And flare to red;

He stands and watches the heavens turning around him,
Watching starlit waters leap and burn
And freeze like seratted [serrated?] teeth tearing the darkness;
Watching the crashing seas heave up like knees
And shake the long sky wall,
And mutter and fall,
And withdraw down the star-edged dark again.

Behind him is the darkness, pushing westward,
Above him mute stars flicker down the air.
These stars, thinks Pierrot, freezing there
Are like so many pilgrims in a forest,
They are like blind people, they are so calm and white.

But you are young, Pierrot; you do not know
That we are souls prisoned between a night and a night;
That we are voiceless pilgrims here alone
Who were once as arrogant in youth as you are,
But now with our spent dreams are overblown.

Look, Pierrot; you, whose winged eyes fly ever before you,
While youth hangs like a bright sword at your side;--
Do you not see the sky on the walls above you,
See you not that your rose which has not died
Is a paper rose? No, you see only the immortals

Upon the shining stairs worn smooth by feet and time.
Look well, Pierrot; there before you are portals
You cannot breach, nor ever hope to climb.

IV.

Above, about the pole star, turn
The constellations, wheeling vaguely down the dim wall of the sky;
Below, at dawn and eve the waters burn,
While only you, Pierrot; you must die;--
You, the silver bow on which the arrow of your life is set.

The shaft is tipped with jade desire, and feathered with your illusions,
The bow is drawn, yet unreleased
For you are not sure, you are still afraid
That you will miss the mark on which the dart is laid.

And so you pause, and watch the sky plain burning
With numberless lanterned pilgrims steadily unreturning;
You hear their solemn singing fill the plain,
You see one pause: his lantern is suddenly darkened,
Then brightly flares, and onward he chants again.

V.

Pierrot sits small and high on a mountain top,
Frosty in carven starlight, stiffly bowed
Lest he knock his head against the stars,
Watching the cliffside seething
With voices beating the air with wings of words

Like blind birds.
The darkness shudders remote with tumultuous breathing.

Pierrot bows his head above his harp
And lets the notes fall slowly through his fingers
Like drops of blood, crimson and sharp:
He shatters a crimson rose of sound on a carpet of upturned faces.
He feels his limbs draw into him with cold
And lets his numb hand fall
Like ice upon his harp: a tinkle of silver,
A whirl of notes about his head grown cold and keen.
They spin and fall, how swiftly they depart!

Pierrot watches the last note fall
Then finds he cannot see o[r] hear at all.
That, says Pierrot, was my heart
That broke and fell away from me
And shattered itself to pieces on the night,
Leaving me frozen, bare of sound and sight.

And, feeling his face freeze into a mask of calmness,
Feeling the sky swim down into his eyes;
Pierrot lifts his face, dumb in starlight,
And raises his arms, and cries
To stars that on clear spokes of silence turn
Hissing into seas that freeze and burn.

VI.

The stars, bright singing faces slowly drawing nearer,

Take their immaculate way across his heart.
Newer voices join the throng, clear and clearer:--
Other pilgrims are waiting to embark
Upon the stagnant ocean overhead.

Pierrot spins and whirls . . . .
Cities beat like surf below him in the dark.
The darkness is a world of lesser worlds
Swiftly spinning in soundless rings of light.

Pierrot spins and whirls
Watching the streaming stars in a narrow pathway
Between rooftops grown snatching and shrill in darkness,

Watching the stars like confetti blown on a wind
Across an open coffin,
Blown like petals in the hair of dancing girls.
He watches the carnival flare and pass
Like a flitting shadow on a glass,
He sees music like rings
Of sound, and breasts of virgins shortening among the rings,
And faces like shattering petals faintly whirl before him.

Torches are smoking circles on cold stars,
Beaten by winds of shouting that gustily rise
About golden gods, about gods of jade and green,
About gods of ivory and glass
And flame clad dancers leaping between.

The shouting dies, the kings depart,
The smoke of torches blows among the stars and soon is gone;
And Pierrot watches the shadows scurry across the street of stone
While above him, crouching, looms the shadow of his heart.

VII.

Pierrot shivers, his soul is a paper lantern
Hung sadly in a garden of dead trees.
His soul, that he once carried so carefully before him
Now gutters and drips: the flames [flame?] is nearly gone
Into the darkness whence it came.
Pierrot rises stiffly, the stone has cramped his knees,---
Thinking that soon his soul will redly vanish in weak flame.

Now that the tumult and shouting has died away
And the music is spun thin along the sky;
He stays alone, he will stay
To watch these strange grey phantoms going by
To grovel in the dust at the doors of palaces.
He stays alone, he will stay
To watch the gusty leaves whip by in darkness
Across the hearts of mortals.

Fainter the music, his eyes grow dim;
The shadows raise their robes and whirl away.
Darkness hastens back and drowns the torches

Lifted like hands to him;
And his own hands, once white, dissolve in grey.

VIII.

Pierrot, sitting chill on a wall in darkness,
Feeling the sharp cold stone stinging his palms,
Seeing the darkness freeze from roof to roof between the houses;--
Stirs, and clasps his arms.
Stars swing back across the empty street,
And ghostly faces are blown like stars across his heart.

Now that the city grows black and chill and empty,---
Who am I, thinks Pierrot, who am I
To stretch my soul out rigid across the sky?

Who am I to chip the silence with footsteps,
Then see the silence fill my steps again?
The wind grows louder about me, shrill with pain,
And blows the petalled faces from my heart.
Shall I stay alone,
Shall I stay alone to watch a dead man pass,
Gibbering at the moon and twisting a paper rose petal by petal apart,----
Or do I see my own face in a glass?

Rather I will watch the stars swing back across the sky
To fill the street like leaves within a coffin;
Fill the hair of old men waiting to die,
While I grow faint upon a wall

Waiting to fall.

It is dark says Pierrot, now that night has come
Rising like an iron wall about me, I am dumb;
I am dumb and huge in starlight,
I am a cliff breaking above a sea in darkness,
I am bound with chains of blue and green;
I am alone in a forest of sound around me
Woven with all beauty that I have felt and seen.

Look, the black bowl of the sky inverted above you
Is chipped at the east, and slowly fills with light;
The stars are whirled and spun like leaves in a porphyry basin

Filling with water, and the night
Sinks and flows and withdraws beyond your sight.

And[;] leaning above his desert sharp with time,
He watches his dream pilgrims singing climb;
He sees them raise their arms upon the sky,
Sees their hands, severed by the horizon,
Glistening and fluttering silently,---
Pierrot stirs, and wakes into a dream.
The desert is empty, turrets and walls in starlight gleam;
Beneath them, multitudes in slumber turn and sigh.

And Pierrot, staring above him into darkness,
Sees shadows and lights and faces before his eyes;

Flitting feet, and hands in a forest of music;
And echoes and perfumes are woven about him
With a silver thread among them, which is pain;--
Pierrot stares into the dark, and sighs,
And enters his dream again.

After the Concert.

The music falls, the light goes up the walls,
Is pooled upon the ceiling
And stirs with lurching shadows reeling
With struggling arms in wraps and overcoats;
Spills on stupid faces blinking eyes,
Then ceilingward is sucked and pooled again.
And we stir and rise,
We take our several ways up crowded aisles
Through veils of scent and stale unmeaning talk;
So we go, with music in our brain,
We hum beneath our breath, we hear again
A dim refrain that haunts us as we go,
Yet which we cannot grasp, and dare not try.

Dusk flows down, and row on row
A spring of lights blooms on a pale green sky,
Is blown from wall to wall and street to street[;]
Across a maze of feet
It weaves, across the smoke of pipe and cigarette.
Arm in arm we walk to this refrain,
This thin elusive phantom in our brain
Which we cannot remember, or forget.

A tide of darkness drowns us, wave by wave,
That lays clear lilac shadows on us,
That sweeps the light from spires, along thin ledges,
That quiets the sharpened roofs which threatened the sunset.
We pause, to raise our joined hands to the far

Still eternal gesture of a star.

So we walk, and dumbly raise our eyes,
Arm in arm in intimate talk;
In a haze of trivialities
We walk, and pause, and walk

In a spring of certainties whitely shattered about us,
To a troubling music oft refrained,
Into the darkness that some day will enfold us, ---
When that is gained, then all is gained.

Weave, you luminous flowers, weave
A gold device upon dark's lowered shield.
We rise, to a hidden music, out of night,
We laugh and weep, and then to night we yield.

Portrait.

Lift your hand between us, dimly raise your face,
And draw the opaque curtains from your eyes.
Let us walk here, softly checked with shadow
And talk of careful trivialities.

Let us lightly speak at random: tonight's movie,
Repeat a broken conversation word for word;
Of friends, and happiness. The darkness falters
While we hear again a music both have heard

Singing blood to blood between our palms.
Come, raise your face, your tiny scrap of mouth

So lightly mobile on your dim white face;
Aloofly talk of life, profound in youth

Yet simple also: young and white and strange
You walk beside me down this shadowed street;
Against my hand your small breast softly lies,
And your laughter breaks the r[h]ythm of our feet.

You are so young. And frankly you believe
This world, this darkened street, this shadowed wall
Are bright with beauty you passionately know
Cannot fade nor cool nor die at all.

Raise your hand, then, to your scarce-seen face

And draw the opaque curtains from your eyes;
Profoundly speak of life, of simple truths,
The while your voice is clear with frank surprise.

The dark ascends
Lightly on pale wings of falling light.
Vague dim wall[s] before us vaguely rise
And then recline again upon faint greenish skies.
Slowly, in a silence pale with violins,
Let us walk where lilacs on the wall
Agitate their hands, and lean and fall[,]
As the darkness deepens, from our sight.

Listen, how once more the silence sings
Between your hands that you so lightly raise
And lay upon me, clear and slim with beauty
Of your nights and days.
Listen . . . Once more this music together we hear,
So slim with faint surprise, and ever near

Between us, as before we saw and heard it,
Rises now in perfect soundless rings.

Place your hand in mine, and lay
Your formless flower face upon the dusk.
Upon this liquid end of day
We float like petals, for we strain
And weakly raise the silence faint with musk,
Then let it fall again.

I see your face through the twilight in my brain,
A dusk of forgotten things, remembered things;
It is a corridor, dark and cool with music,
Too dim for sight,
That leads me to a door which brings
You, clothed in quiet sound for my delight.

Let us go, then; you and I, while evening grows
And a delicate violet thins the rose
That stains the sky;
We will go alone there, you and I,
And watch the trees step naked from the shadow
Like women shrugging upward from their gowns.

No, be silent, do not speak at all.
Watch this silver star grow pale and drown;
See, the ripples of its fall
Wrinkle the pool's face in concealing smiles.
Does it smile at us? we raise our heads.
Across your face the shadow of your smile
Trembles in your eyes like rain upon two pools.
You look at me, and raise your mouth, and form

The silence in the image of a word.

Lift your hand and touch your hair
Simply parted backward from your face
Like wings; and let the silence place
And weave our dreams like lilacs in your hair.

[A Symphony]

The dark ascends
On golden wings of violins
And lights, on music softly played
As if the shadow fingers strayed
Upon the soft moon's silver strings.
Then, as all silence smoothly sings,
Rise the quickening silver chimes,
And in pursuit there swiftly climbs
A slender flute, a clarinet;
A graceful scented faint regret
As muted violins rise again,
Threading with thin silver pain
A golden weave of solemn horn.

Pulse, you timbrels, flare and knock.
The gusty stars, in flock on flock,
Draw the moon across the world[.]
Rise, you shrill pipes, twist and whirl

Above these chill hands linked in dance
To this - called life - extravagance.
Shudder drum, and mutter horn
Beneath this dark whence all are born,
Below this dark whence all return,
Clays that freeze, clays that burn!
That rise from dust and walk to dust
Where beauty cries, and falls in lust.
Come, you far winds, rise and whirl
This scattered dead dust from the world.

A febrile motion now is mazed
Upon this dark where we have gazed
And sought a thing that we found fair,
And yet found nought save darkness there;
Beneath a song that, though we heard,
Distinguished not a single word;
A 'why' and 'whence' we never knew
As violins rose and fell and flew.

We dance and dance, the while our faces
Lighten, darken, resume their places
By walls of dark where spikes of bloom
Like censers swing, and wall the room
With scented mirrors that beguile
Us with the promise of a smile [line canceled]
Which time alone can now efface;
Which always will return a face
When we draw near, to stir each heart
With memories ere we touch and part.
Harps soothe darkness to appease
The nervous swiftness of our knees
That maze the dark with little lights
To twinkle beyond all empty nights
When we are old, and lonely and wise,
And think and smile, with shadows in our eyes.

Pulse, you timbrels, flare and knock.
The gusty stars, in flock on flock,

Draw the moon across the world.
Rise, you shrill pipes, twist and whirl
Above these chill hands linked in dance
To this - called life - extravagance.
Shudder drum, and mutter horn
Beneath the dark whence all are born,
Below the dark whence all return,
Clays that freeze, clays that burn!
That rise from dust and walk to dust
Where beauty cries, and falls in lust.
Come, you far winds, rise and whirl
This scattered dead dust from the world.

. . . .

The music pauses, to remark
The broken silence fall in dark,
Then the silence slow ascends
On golden wings of violins,
On flute and harp, on clarinet,
To a scented faint regret.

Our shadows merge, then we begin
The dance of harp and violin.
The music sighs and gropes and sings;
While we, as if on silver wings,
Whirl around the dark's slow flame
In a breathless heartless game
Of hunter and quarry, a febrile whirl
Above the dark where lurks the world;
Within these safe walls we have raised
And beyond which we have never gazed
Into the forest of hungry stone
Where so many dreams are blown
Like leaves, like stars along the sky;
In a breathless game so soon to die
When these safe deep-rooted walls
Go crashing down, and darkness falls.

Faint and sharp and swift and thin
Go harp and flute and violin;
These luminous limbs that through the dark

Shed each its light, its short[-]lived spark
From each motion woven life;
Each brilliant spark that springs from strife,
Is shed from pain, lives but to dance
To this strange sweet extravagance
Until it falls, cold of pain
And lightless, into dark again.

Swift and thin and faint and sharp
This dance of violin, flute and harp;
The whole of life with motion mazed,
A tiny face where each has gazed
As it burned brighter, motion fanned;
And each tiny spark of hand
A moment held, then blown to dark
And silence with the face's spark.

Swiftly whirl then, till these walls
Go crashing down, and darkness falls;
Swiftly dance then, little elves,
You are the sparks within our selves;
The delicate f[i]re within the clay
That some day life will blow away
From each of us; and when alone
We grope beneath cold crumbled stone,
[shall]
We will [canceled] hear the voices, ghostly thin,
Of harp and flute and violin.

[Several lines of illegible handwriting]

Rain, rain . . . a field of silver grain
Grown up to the sky.
Rain, rain . . . in a caverned brain.
The sleeper stirs, and sleepily opens an eye.
From wall to wall, down to the nethermost tower,
Bells on golden wings slide lightly down.
An hour, another hour
Is stripped from time, discarded on the ground.

He lies and listens, while the bells
Echo his life away. The ghostly sea
Rises and walks on feet of muffled sound,
Shakes the darkness where he lies and tosses;
Then the bells again.

Rain, rain . . . bell to lower bell
Lowered and fell, and fell, and fell.
Remember, remember . . .
Life is not a passing: it is an endless repeating.
Tomorrow you rise, draw your curtains,
And at your window, sadly staring down,
See the stars, your only permanent beauty
Pale with the sinking dark, and drown;
See a thousand petty things arise before you,
Find another wrinkle in your mirror, turn away
As you saw, and turned there yesterday.

Remember, remember . . .
As dust you rose, as dust you someday fall
In spite of all your troubled, futile tossing
Of tortured hands above this ancient wall.

Remember, how your life, grown clear and clearer,
[Led]
Lead [canceled] you along sharp peaks where cities gleam;
[Led]
Lead [canceled] you into the desert of your heart, to seek there
A substance which you found was shadow, dream;
Remember, that from this road there is no returning
No matter what perplexities star your sky;
Remember, life discards you, yet never changes:
Where men have cried once, men will always cry.

Once on a sea shore, saltily grey,
He stood. Sharp hands of wind

Ran over him, tugged at his clothing,
Paused to stare into his eyes,
Then ran behind to pull at his clothes again.

Dust you rose, as dust you someday fall . .
Above his head the tall sea shook its wall
And broken bits of it swirled to his feet
Upon small waves, and broke again, and rattled there.

It is strange, he thought, pushing at the wind's face with his hand;
How even when alone, like this, I stand
There is always something near, some scarce remembered thing
That comes, I know not whence, to strip and change
This lonely calm where I would walk.
Even here these vacuous birds of talk

Of 'you' and 'me' come crying down the wind. It, he thought, is strange.

It is strange, he thought, and stood beneath a sky as white as salt,
Fondling a pebble, smooth and heavy, that he tossed and caught;
How nothing is accomplished in this life,
How all our cherished labors time will crumble, change:
We build our houses, block by block, in pain
For our children to pull down, then build them up again.
He watched his rock hiss in the sea and thought it strange.

At his feet small waves hissed, spread and died. . . .

Dust you rose, as dust you some day fall
No matter how your soul, from wall to wall
Cries and whirrs and clings. . . .
The sea smoldered among the pebbles at his feet,
The sea edge whitely curled, as paper burns,
And foamed the shifting sand in slow pulsations.

Small waves hissed up against his side
And columned moonlight fell and broke from wave to wave,
Shattered again upon the beach, and sank.
He lay at lenght [length?], saw his wet body gleam
As the tongues of sea ran over it;
He felt the waves beneath him flow and part,

And then like hair about his body stream.

It is strange, he thought, watching a far light blinking,
How all our life is futile, thwarted dream;
Like that light, beating frail wings on the dark,
Like these waves that on this dark sand stream.
It is strange, that I should lie here thinking;
For some day all of us, light, waves and all
Will feel the sea of darkness softly touch us,
And one by one in darkness we will fall.

And he lay, and watched his inert hand
Like a forgotten seaweed on the sand

And thought: We beat our hands on walls of blind despair,
We raise our palms to stars in clear slow air
Yet touch them not: they are not stars we see;
We cannot know, we only grope and stare
At restless lights reflected in the sea.

Dark drew slowly nearer on the sand
And, as he slept, it filled his eyes;
And the sea approached and ran its hand
Lightly along his limbs and back and thighs.

Love Song.

Shall I walk, then, through a corridor of profundities
Carefully erect (I am taller that [than?] I look)
To a certain door - - - and shall I dare
To open it? I smoothe my mental hair
With an oft changed phrase that I revise again
Until I have forgotten what it was at first;
Settle my tie with: I have brought a book,
Then seat myself with: We have passed the worst.

Then I shall sit among careful cups of tea,
Aware of a slight perspiring as to brow,
(The smell of scented cigarettes will always trouble me) ;

I shall sit, so patently at ease,
Stiffly erect, decorous as to knees
Among toy balloons of dignity on threads of talk.

And do I dare
(I once more stroke my hand across my hair)
But the window of my mind flies shut, I am in a room
Of surcharged conversation, and of jewelled hands;
- - -Here one slowly strips a flower stalk.
It is too close in here, I rise and walk,
Firmly take my self-possession by the hand.

Now, do I dare,
Who sees the light gleam on her intricate hair?
Shall I assume a studied pose, or shall I stand - - - - -

Oh, Mr. . . .? You are so kind . . . .
Again the door slams inward on my mind.

Not at all . . . .

Replace a cup,
Return and pick a napkin up.

My tongue, a bulwark where a last faint self-possession hides,
Fails me: I withdraw, retreat,
Conscious of the glances on my feet,
And feel as if I trod in sand.

Yet I may raise my head a little while.
The world revolves behind a painted smile.

And now, while evening lies embalmed upon the west
And a last faint pulse of life fades down the sky,
We will go alone, my soul and I,
To a hollow cadence down this neutral street;
To a rythm of feet
Now stilled and fallen. I will walk alone,
The uninvited one who dares not go
Whither the feast is spread to friend and foe,
Whose courage balks the last indifferent gate,
Who dares not join the beggars at the arch of stone.

Change and change: the world revolves to worlds,

To minute whorls
And particles of soil on careless thumbs.
Now I shall go alone,
I shall echo streets of stone, while evening comes
Treading space and beat, space and beat.
The last left seed of beauty in my heart
That I so carefully tended, leaf and bloom,
Falls in darkness.

But enough. What is all beauty? What, that I
Should raise my hands palm upward to the sky,
That I should weakly tremble and fall dumb
At some cryptic promise or pale gleam;--
A sudden wing, a word, a cry?

Evening dies, and now that night has come
Walking still streets, monk-like, grey and dumb;
Then softly clad in grey, lies down again;
I also rise and walk, and die in dream,
For dream is death, and death but fathomed dream.

And shall I walk these streets while passing time
Softly ticks my face, my thinning hair?
I should have been a priest in floorless halls
Wearing his eyes thin on a faded manuscript.

The world revolves. High heels and scented shawls,
Painted masks, and kisses mouth and mouth:

Gesture of a senile pantaloon
To make us laugh.

I have measured time, I measured time
With span of thumb and finger
As one who seeks a bargain: sound enough
I think, but slightly worn;
There's still enough to cover me from cold,
Momentous indecisions, change
And loneliness. Does not each fold
Repeat - - the while I measure time, I measure time - -
The word, the thought, the soundless empty gesture
Of him that it so bravely once arrayed?

Spring . . . shadowed walls, and kissing in the dark.
I, too; was young upon a time, I too; have felt

All life, at one small word, within me melt;
And strange slow swooning wings I could not see
Stirring the beautiful silence over me.

I grow old, I grow old.
Could I walk within my garden while the night
Comes gently down,
And see the garden maidens dancing, white
And dim, across the flower beds?

I would take cold: I dare not try,
Nor watch the stars again born in the sky
Eternally young.

I grow old, I grow old.
Submerged in the firelight's solemn gold
I sit, watching the restless shadows, red and brown,

Float there till I disturb them, then they drown.

I measure time, I measure time.
I see my soul, disturbed, awake and climb
A sudden dream, and fall
And whimpering, crowd near me in the dark.

And do I dare, who steadily builds a wall
Of hour on hour, and day, then lifts a year
That heavily falls in place, while time
Ticks my face, my thinning hair, my heart
In which a faint last long remembered beauty hides?

I should have been a priest in floorless halls
Whose hand, worn thin by turning endless pages,

Lifts, and strokes his face, and falls
And stirs a dust of time heaped grain on grain,
Then gropes the book, and turns it through again;

Who turns the pages through, who turns again,
While darkness lays soft fingers on his eyes
And strokes the lamplight from his brow, to wake him, and he dies.

The Dancer.

I am Youth, so swift, so white and slim,
Who haunts you, tempts you, bids you fly
Across this floor of polished porphyry,
To raise your arms, to try and clasp my knees.

You are Youth? Yet you cannot appease
This flame that, like a music from your hair,
Sheds through me as though I were but air;
That strips me bare, my sudden life reveals.

Yes, I will hurt you, as my tiny heels
- - -That you could cup in your two hands, and still- - -
Have mazed your life against your will

With restless little flames, like mercury, like [gold(?)]

You have mazed my life with swiftness, for I hold
The phantom that I thought was you, and find
That you have flown like music, and my mind
Like water, wrinkles back where your face mirrored was.

I am Youth. White sprays of stars
Crowned me, shattering fell, while my slight music played;
And your heart, like lips where my clear lips were laid,
Parts, and silence lays its hand on them.

Laxly reclining, he watches the firelight going
Across the ceiling, down the farther wall
In cumulate waves, a golden river flowing
Above them both, down yawning dark to fall
Like music dying down a monstrous brain.
Laxly reclining, he sees her sitting there
With the firelight like a hand laid on her hair,
With the firelight like a hand upon the keys
Playing a music of lustrous muted gold.
Bathed in gold she sits, upon her knees
Her languid hands, palm upward, lie at ease,
Filling with gold at each flame's spurting rise,
Spilling gold as each flame sinks and dies;

Watching her plastic shadow on the wall
In unison with the firelight lift and fall,
To the music by the firelight played
Upon the keys from which her hands had strayed
And fallen.

A pewter bowl of lilacs in the room
Seem [seems?] to him to weigh and change the gloom
Into a palpable substance he can feel
Heavily on his hands, slowing the wheel
The firelight steadily turns upon the ceiling.
The firelight steadily hums, steadily wheeling
Until his brain, stretched and tautened, suddenly cracks.

["]Play something else.["]

And laxly sees his brain
Whirl to infinite fragments, like brittle stars,
Vortex together again, and whirl again.

["]Play something else.["]

He tries to keep his tone
Lightly natural, watching the shadows thrown,
Watching the timid shadows near her throat
Link like hands about her from the dark.
His eyes like hurried fingers fumble and fly
About the narrow bands with which her dress is caught
And lightly trace the line of back and thigh.
He sees his brain disintegrate, spark by spark.

["]Play something else,["] he says.

And on the dark
His brain floats like a moon behind his eyes;
Swelling, retreating enormously. He shuts them
As one concealed suppresses two loud cries
And on the troubled dark a vision sees.

It is as if he watched her mount a stair
And rose with her on the suppleness of her knees,
And saw her skirts in swirling line on line,
Saw the changing shadows ripple and rise
After the flexing muscles; subtle thighs,
[h]
Rythm of back and throat and gathered train.

A bursting moon, wheels spin in his brain.
What was that? That rushing of harsh rain?
He walks his life, and reaching the end,
He turns it as one turns a wall.

. . . . .

She plays, and softly playing, sees the room
Dissolve, and like a dream the grey walls fade
And sink, while music, softly played,
Softly flows through lilac[-]scented gloom.
She is a flower lightly cast
Upon a river flowing, dimly going
Between two silent shores where willows lean,
Watching the moon stare through the cherry screen.

A clamor of endless waves against the dark,
A swiftly thunderous surf, swiftly retreating.
His brain falls hissing from him, a spark, a spark[,]
And his eyes like hurried fingers fumble and fly
Among the timid shadows near her throat,
About the narrow bands with which her dress is caught,
And lightly trace the line of back and thigh.
He sees his brain disintegrate, spark by spark[,]
And she turns as if she heard two cries.

He stands and watches her mount the stair
Step by step, with her subtle suppleness,

This nervous strength that was ever his surprise;
The lifted throat[,] the thin crisp swirl of dress
Like a ripple of naked muscles before his eyes.
A bursting moon: wheels spin in his brain,
Shrieking against sharp walls of sanity,
And whirl in a vortex of sparks together again.
At the turn she stops, and shivers there,
And hates him as he steadily mounts the stair.

Orpheus.

Here he stands, while eternal evening falls
And it is like a dream between grey walls
Dimly falling, dimly falling
Between tw [two?] walls of shrunken topless stone,
Between two walls with silence on them grown.
Here he stands, in a litter of leaves upon the floor;
In a solemn silver of scattered springs,
Among the smooth green buds before the door
He stands and sings.
The twilight is severed with waters always falling,
And heavy with budded flowers that never die;
And a voice ever calling, ever calling,

Sweetly and soberly.

I am she who, one among numberless faces,
Bent to you, to the music you softly played;
Who walked with you, hand in hand, in many places
And followed you through forests unafraid.
I am she who, woven in the rain,
Swayed to the, music you had played on me;
Who laid cool hands on you, who sang with a thousand mouths . . . .
He hears the voice, he hears the voice again- - -
I am she! I am she!

Spring stirs the walls of a cold street,
Sowing silver seeds of pain in frozen places;

Across meadows like simply smiling quiet faces,
Across wrinkled streams, and grass that knew her feet.

These dreams, unstilled, rise lightly from his brain
To dimly walk by walls of marbled sound,
And then lie down again.

I am he who, ringed about with faces,
Stared on a spectral darkness stiff with eyes.
I raise my hand in a darkness stagnant with faces,
I break thin violin threads of cries
As softly I go where together we walked and dreamed.

I am he who[,] sick with beauty, streamed
Across the dark, and crossed the dark.
Restless limbs of shadow beside me tossed and gleamed.
I am the brain that, lying on the ground,
Flowered in tenebrous wisps upon the dark.

These dreams, unstilled, lightly rise in pain
To dimly walk by walls of marbled sound,
And then lie down again.

And I, raised by shadow hands,
Go softly where together we walked and dreamed
To a music on our joined flesh calmly played.
Shadow limbs turn in ghostly sarabands
And their hands touch me as her hands touched and strayed.

I am he, I am he
Who raised his palms for rain;
Whose dreams, so dimly walking, dimly reclining,
Now rise and walk again.

And I, who walked in memoried spring,
Who saw her shadowed eyes and lifted throat
Sweetly well with laughter and overflow;
I am the hands in which this gold was caught;
I am he who heard her sing,
Who saw her gently graven, and I go
Where these dreams, once stilled, now lightly rise in pain
And turn and grow, and then lie down again.

I am he, I am he

Who, across the dark and across the dark,
Wove a slender net with thread of pain
To snare a ghost of rain.
I am he who, sleepless, staring down,
Saw shadows crossing marbled walls of sound:
A sea in which I sink, yet cannot drown.

I am he, I am he
Who raised his palms for rain;
Whose dreams, so dimly walking, dimly reclining,
Now rise and walk again.

Here he stands, while eternal evening falls
And it is like a dream between grey walls
Dimly falling, dimly falling
Between two walls of shrunken topless stone,

Between two walls with silence on them grown.
Here he stands, in a litter of leaves upon the floor,
In a solemn silver of scattered springs;
Among the smooth green buds before the door
He stands and sings.

Philosophy.

There is no shortening[-]breasted nymph to shake
The thickets that stem up the lidless blaze
Of sunlight stiffening the shadowed ways,
Nor does the haunted silence ever wake
Nor ever stir.

No footfall trembles in the smoky brush
Where bright leaves flicker down the dappled shade,
A tapestry that cloaks an empty glade,
And quivers up to still the pulsing thrush
[A(?)]nd frighten her

With the contact of its chilly hands
Until she falls, and melts into the hight [night? height?]
Among the cedars[,] splashing on the light[,]

That crowd the folded darkness as it stands
About each grave,

Whose headstone glimmers dimly in the gloom,
Threaded by the doves' unquiet calls,
Like memories that swim between the walls
And dim the peopled stillness of a room
Into a nave

Where no light breaks the thin cool panes of glass,
To fall like butterflies upon the floor;
While the shadows crowd within the door
And whisper in the dead leaves as they pass
Along the ground.

Here the sunset paints its wheeling gold
Where there is no breast to still in strife
Of joy and sadness, nor does any life
Flame the hills and vales grown thin and cold
        And bare of sound.

April.

Somewhere a slender voiceless breeze will go,
Unlinking the poplars' hands
And ruffling the pool's face quietly below
Where each clump of hazel stands,
Clad in its own simply parted hair;
And mirrored half in sleep and half awake
And casting slender white hands on
The pool's breast, dreaming there to slake
The thirsty alders pausing in the dawn.
Here the hidden violets first appear.

Somewhere a blackbird, slowly wheeling,
Draws endless narrowing circles on the sky
Above each brake, timidly kneeling,
Upon the stream's bank, watching breathlessly

And quaking to itself within the deep
Pool. Here the young leaves shy appear
And cling to the hazel arms like silver sleeves
Simply crossed, shaken with fear,
While their light about the hazels w[ea]ves
A spell on them to still their restless sleep.

Some ways are white with birches in a hood
Of tender green. A sunset weaves
A tapestry upon some silent wood,
Calmly quiet, and the leaves
Clothe the half[-]clad trees in solemn gold.
Somewhere a girl goes, slender white,
While sunset swims in her eyes' pool[,]
To meet her shepherd ere the night
Descends on clear dark wings to lull and cool

And dim the world in brooding fold on fold.

Somewhere the stars in silent rows
Spring and blossom in the turning sky,
While a nightingale's song blows
And, soaring upward, shatters silverly
Against the narrow moon. In dim-lit ways
A sighing wind shakes in its grasp
A straight resilient poplar in the mist,
Until its reaching hands unclasp,
And then the wind and sky bend down, and kiss
Its simple, cool whitely breathless face.

(end)

APPENDIX A

List of Known Versions of Poems in *Vision in Spring*

Joseph Blotner describes the physical appearance of *Vision in Spring* as follows (Joseph Blotner, letter, 9 June 1983):

[1] Cover: "board covered with brownish-green paper, mottled like an amoeba or cell-slide. Sheets were stapled together and white paper was pasted inside of covers. The spine was covered with white parchment or vellum and the title (a square of linen paper pasted on) was lettered in india ink."

[2] 6 unnumbered blank pages (3 sheets) before title page

[3] Title page

[4] Verso of title page (blank)

[5] Contents page

[6] Verso (blank)

[7] 2 more blank pages (1 sheet)

Faulkner's pagination:

1–5 "Vision in Spring"

a. "Vision in Spring," 5 pp. photocopy of carbon typescript, 52 lines. This is *Vision in Spring* I, pp. 1–5. See Keen Butterworth, "A Census of Manuscripts and Typescripts of William Faulkner's Poetry," *Mississippi Quarterly* 26 (Summer 1973): 333–359, Published Poetry, number 69 for prior listing of *b* and *d*.

b. "Visions in Spring," *Contempo* 1 (1 February 1932): 1 (52 lines).

c. "Vision in Spring," 3 pp. typescript with two holograph corrections, stanzas 2–5 repeated and stanzas 8–11 repeated but canceled. Final stanza varies from *b*, University of Virginia (UVa).

d. "Vision in Spring," 3 pp. typescript, Humanities Research Center, University of Texas, Austin (UT). Has one holograph correction in ink.

6–9 "Interlude"

a. "Interlude," 4 pp. photocopy of carbon typescript, 49 lines. This is *Vision in Spring* II, pp. 6–9. See Butterworth, "Census," Unpublished Poetry, number 18 for prior listing of *b* and *c*.

b. "Interlude," 3 pp. typescript identical to *Vision in Spring* version other than some changes in punctuation, UT.

c. "Interlude," 2 pp. typescript fragment, 46 lines visible, 28 lines complete. Has "5." in ink above title, UT. See Appendix B.

10–29 "The World and Pierrot. A Nocturne."

a. "The World and Pierrot. A Nocturne," 18 pp. photocopy of carbon typescript, 224 lines. This is *Vision in Spring* III, pp. 10–29. See Butterworth, "Census," Published Poetry, number 45 for prior listing of *b* and *c*.

b. "Nocturne," *The Ole Miss, 1920–1921* XXV: 214–215, lines 29–50 of *a* with 11 variants. Reproduced in James B. Meriwether, *The Literary Career of William Faulkner: A Bibliographical Study*, Figure 2.

c. "Nocturne," Carvel Collins, ed., *Early Prose and Poetry of William Faulkner*, pp. 82–83. Both *b* and *c*, which are listed in Butterworth, "Census," are part 2 of this eight-part poem (pp. 12–14 in *VIS*).

30–32 "After the Concert"

a. "After the Concert," 3 pp. photocopy of carbon typescript, 39 lines. This is *Vision in Spring* IV, pp. 30–32.

b. "So we walk and dumbly raise our eyes," first line, 1 p. typescript: burned fragment, 12 lines complete, UT (Butterworth, "Census," Unidentified Fragments, number 50).

c. "After the Concert," 1 p. typescript, "4." in ink above title: burned fragment, first 21 lines visible, 14 complete, UT (Butterworth, "Census," Unpublished Poetry, number 3). See Appendix B.

33–35 "Portrait"

a. "Portrait," 3 pp. photocopy of carbon typescript, 24 lines. This is *Vision in Spring* V, pp. 33–35. See Butterworth, "Census," Published Poetry, number 52 for prior listing of *b–d*.

b. "Portrait," *Double Dealer* 3 (June 1922): 337, 24 lines, 14 variants.

c. "Portrait," Collins, *Early Prose and Poetry* (identical to *b*), pp. 99–100.

d. "Portrait," 1 p. typescript: burned fragment, 19 lines visible, 13 complete, "3." in ink above title, UT.

36–39 Untitled, VI

a. Untitled, 4 pp. photocopy of carbon typescript, 47 lines. This is *Vision in Spring* VI, pp. 36–39.

b. "The dark ascends," first line, 1 p. typescript: burned fragment, 22 lines visible, 16 complete, UT (Butterworth, "Census," Unidentified Fragments, number 18). Typescript has arabic numeral "6." above poem.

c. "Let us go alone, then, you and I, while evening grows," first line, 1 p. typescript: burned fragment, 19 lines visible, 15 complete, UT.

d. "Your eyes like rain upon two pools," first complete line, 1 p. typescript: burned fragment (variant) of last 2 strophes, 15 lines visible, first 4 incomplete. At end of poem is typed "William Faulkner. / July 1920." See Appendix B.

40–46 Untitled, VII; "A Symphony" penciled at top of p. 40, not William Faulkner's hand.

a. Untitled, 7 pp. photocopy of carbon typescript, 115 lines, line 41 canceled but legible and illegible lines written at bottom of p. 46. This is *Vision in Spring* VII, pp. 40–46.

b. "Symphony," 4 pp. typescript: burned fragment, 88 lines visible, 71 complete, UT (Butterworth, "Census," Unpublished Poetry, number 33).

c. Untitled, 1 p. typescript: burned fragment, third and part of fourth strophe visible, 24 lines visible, 16 complete, UT (Butterworth, "Census," Unidentified Fragments, number 41).

d. Untitled, 1 p. typescript: burned fragment, 25 lines visible, 22 complete, UT.

e. "Like leaves, like stars along the sky," first line, 1 p. typescript: burned fragment, sixth and parts of fifth and seventh strophes, 22 lines visible, 13 complete, UT.

f. "Pulse, you timbrels, flare and knock," first line, second stanza, 1 p. typescript: burned fragment, 23 lines visible, 17 complete, UT (Butterworth, "Census," Unidentified Fragments, number 41).

g. Untitled, 1 p. typescript: burned fragment, 24 lines visible, 22 complete, UT (Butterworth, "Census," Unidentified Fragments, number 41).

47–54 Untitled, VIII

a. Untitled, 8 pp. photocopy of carbon typescript, 92 lines. This is *Vision in Spring* VIII, pp. 47–54. It appears to be a unique copy. I found no other versions in any of the Faulkner collections consulted. Lines 30–31 have overstrike and penciled correction "Led."

55–64 "Love Song"

a. "Love Song," 9 pp. photocopy of carbon typescript, 116 lines. This is *Vision in Spring* IX, pp. 55–64. In his "Census," Unpublished Poetry, number 28, Butterworth calls the "Love Song" fragments at UT Faulkner's "Prufrock poem." There are 29 pp. of typescript fragments of a poem similar to "Love Song"; of these, 23 sheets have holograph drafts of *Vision in Spring* IX on versos. See Appendix B.

65–66 "The Dancer"

a. "The Dancer," 2 pp. photocopy of carbon typescript, 20 lines. This is *Vision in Spring* X, pp. 65–66.

b. "The Dancer," 1 p. typescript: 20 lines in quatrains, beneath the title is typed "to V. de G. F." (Faulkner's step-daughter), UVa.

c. "Your bonds are strong as steel, but soft--," first complete line, 1 p. typescript: burned fragment, 9 lines visible, 8 complete in quatrains, UT (Butterworth, "Census," Unidentified Fragments, number 60).

67–75 Untitled, XI; "Marriage" in another draft.

a. Untitled, 9 pp. photocopy of carbon typescript, 102 lines. This is *Vision in Spring* XI, pp. 67–75. See Butterworth, "Census," Published Poetry, number 40 for prior listing of *b–f*.
b. "Marriage," 4 pp. typescript with one holograph correction, UVa. This is *A Green Bough* II (1933).
c. "Marriage," 4 pp. typescript, University of Mississippi Library (Rowanoak Papers).
d. Untitled, 1 p. typescript: burned fragment, 16 lines visible, 12 complete, UT.
e. Untitled, 1 p. typescript: burned fragment, 17 lines visible, 11 complete, UT.
f. Untitled, 1 p. typescript: burned fragment, 13 lines visible, 10 complete, UT.

76–82 "Orpheus"

a. "Orpheus," 7 pp. photocopy of carbon typescript, 79 lines. This is *Vision in Spring* XII, pp. 76–82. See Butterworth, "Census," Published Poetry, number 49.
b. "Orpheus," 2 pp. typescript: burned fragments, 43 lines visible, 40 complete, Beinecke Library, Yale University. See Appendix B.
c. *A Green Bough* XX is composed of the first 13 lines and lines 23–36 of *Vision in Spring* "Orpheus."

83–85 "Philosophy"

a. "Philosophy," 3 pp. photocopy of carbon typescript, 30 lines. This is *Vision in Spring* XIII, pp. 83–85. See Butterworth, "Census," Published Poetry, number 50.
b. "Philosophy," 2 pp. typescript, 30 lines with one pencil correction apparently not in Faulkner's hand, UVa. This is *A Green Bough* V.
c. Untitled, 1 p. typescript: burned fragment, 17 lines visible, 14 complete, UT.
d. Untitled, 1 p. typescript: burned fragment, part of 1 line visible, UT.
e. Untitled, 1 p. typescript: burned fragment, parts of 4 lines visible, UT.
f. Untitled, 1 p. typescript: burned fragment, parts of 5 lines visible, UT.
g. Untitled, 1 p. typescript: burned fragment, parts of 14 lines visible, UT.
h. Untitled, 1 p. typescript carbon: burned fragment, 15 lines visible, 1 complete, UT. Has holograph instructions in the right margin.
i. Untitled holograph manuscript: burned fragment, last 4 lines are also in *a*, UT.

86–88 "April"

a. "April," 3 pp. photocopy of carbon typescript, 40 lines. This is *Vision in Spring* XIV, pp. 86–88. At bottom of p. 88 in parentheses is typed "(end)." Also see Butterworth, "Census," Published Poetry, number 6.

b. "April," *Contempo* 1 (1 February 1932): 2.

c. "April," 2 pp. typescript, UVa.

d. Untitled, 1 p. typescript: burned fragment, 22 lines visible, 18 complete, UT.

e. Untitled, 1 p. typescript: burned fragment, 11 lines visible, 9 complete, UT.

f. Untitled, 1 p. typescript: burned fragment, second and fragments of first and third strophes, 20 lines visible, 18 complete, UT.

Unnumbered pages:

[89] Blank end page with Faulkner's holograph note in india ink on rebinding.

[90] Verso (blank). No flyleaves between it and cover.

APPENDIX B
Vision in Spring Fragments

Included in this appendix are fragments of versions of poems in *Vision in Spring*. Excepting the "Orpheus" fragment, which belongs to the Collection of American Literature, the Beinecke Library, Yale University, these versions are part of the Faulkner Collection at the Humanities Research Center, University of Texas at Austin. Thanks are due to Ellen Dunlap, Cathy Henderson, and John Kirkpatrick at the HRC and to the library staff at Yale for help in assembling these fragments and to both institutions and to Jill Faulkner Summers for permission to reproduce them here.

5

Interlude.

Once more a soft-starred evening falls
Upon these empty streets and walls;
Once more the world sinks into dark, he said,
Watching calm gusts of stars swept overhead
Like candle flames across a coffin blown---
And leaves a flare of light to whisper ancient stone.

Restless branches gestured on the dark
Above him; roof-peaks, narrow, black and stark
Like sharpened foreheads, streamed with star-bright hair.
Someday he, too, must die. The air
Swung with the swinging trees above him, shadows tossed,
Futilely gestured, fell, in dark were lost.

I will watch them through clear glass
Of polished silence, wearily enter there----
[illegible] and green dusk: they pass
[illegible] of their hair
[illegible] saraband
[illegible] coral sand.
[illegible] urn
[illegible] hair [illegible]

On this two-page fragment (a version of "Interlude," VIS *II, lines 1–18 and 28–46) the numbering has been changed, suggesting that it was also used in another sequence (possibly* Orpheus, and Other Poems*).*

Solemnly the clear fantastic reed
Clearly repeats a dark and simple need
Of someone, something, some still unfound bliss
To bless in quiet pain, and kiss.

Slowly, solemnly, and turn
Across the world's dumb darkly dreaming face.
Raise your pipes: the melodies repeat
The calm majestic maze of dewy feet;
Solemnly the clear fantastic pipes refrain
The movement, solemnly again
The simple melodies repeat.

Slowly, solemnly, and turn.
Raise your face grown calm and sad, your eyes,
Raise your mouth that seeks and sings and sighs
[illegible] of s[illegible]e untasted bliss
[illegible] pain, and kiss. . . .

[illegible] te and clang.
[illegible] ness that once rang
[illegible] eave up like [illegible]

Like the next fragment, "After the Concert," VIS *IV, this poem was typed with a black ribbon. The poem number is in black ink and probably not in Faulkner's hand. In the extant lines, the author made only minor word changes (lines 15 and 45) and changes in punctuation (lines 14, 31, and 46).*

4

After the Concert.

The music falls, the light goes up the walls,
Is pooled upon the ceiling
And stirs with lurching shadows wheeling
With struggling arms in wraps and overcoats;
Spills on stupid faces blinking eyes,
Then ceilingward is sucked and pooled again.
And we stir and rise,
We take our several ways up crowded aisles
Through veils of scent and stale unmeaning talk;
So we go with music in our brain,
We hum beneath the breath, we hear again
A dim refrain that haunts us as we go
Yet which we cannot grasp, and dare not try.

Dusk flows down, and row on row
A spring of [illegible]hts blooms on a pale green sky,
[illegible] wall and street to street---

[illegible] smoke of pipe and cigarette.
[illegible] refrain,
[illegible]n our brain
[illegible] forget.

On this one-page black-ribbon typescript fragment (a version of "After the Concert," VIS *IV, lines 1–21) the poem number, also in black ink, is unchanged. In the fourteen complete lines are one word change (line 3) and two punctuation changes (lines 12 and 15).*

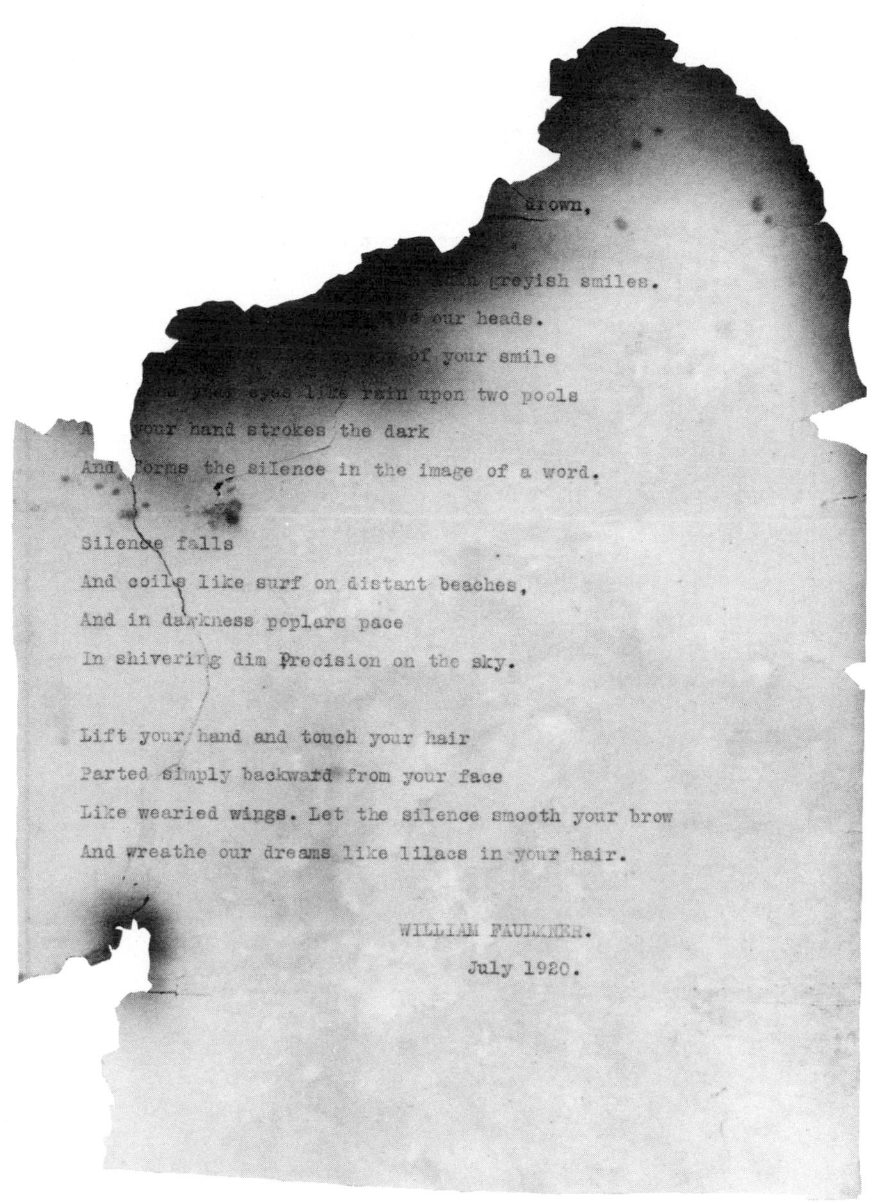

drown,

greyish smiles.

our heads.

your smile

rain upon two pools

your hand strokes the dark

And forms the silence in the image of a word.

Silence falls
And coils like surf on distant beaches,
And in darkness poplars pace
In shivering dim Precision on the sky.

Lift your hand and touch your hair
Parted simply backward from your face
Like wearied wings. Let the silence smooth your brow
And wreathe our dreams like lilacs in your hair.

WILLIAM FAULKNER.
July 1920.

This dated black-ribbon typescript fragment appears to be a version of the last twelve lines of VIS *VI. Four of its lines are unique: "Silence falls / And coils like surf on distant beaches, / And in darkness poplars pace / In shivering dim Precision on the sky."*

ORPHEUS.

Here he stands, while eternal evening falls
And it is like a dream between grey walls
Dimly falling, dimly falling
Between two walls of shrunken topless stone,
Between two walls with silence on them grown.
Here he stands, in a litter of leaves upon the floor,
In a solemn silver of scattered springs;
Among the smooth green buds upon the door
He stands and sings.

Spring stirs the walls of a cold street,
Sowing silver seeds of pain in frozen places;
Across meadows like simply sailing quiet faces,
Across wrinkled streams, and grass that knew her feet.

I am he who, ringed about with faces,
Stare on a spectral darkness stiff with eyes;
I raise my hand in a twilight stagnant with faces,
I break thin violin threads of cries
As alone I go where together once we strayed.
Shadow limbs turn in silver sarabands
touch me as her hands touched and play

And I, who walk in memoried spring,
Who saw her shadowed eyes and lifted throat
Sweetly well with laughter, and overflow:
I am the hands in which this gold was gaught.
The twilight is severed with waters always falling,
And heavy with budded flowers that never die;
And her voice is ever calling, ever calling,
Sweetly and soberly.

I am he, I am he
Who raises his palms for rain;
Whose dream, dimly walking, dimly reclining,
Rises and walks again.

Here he stands, while eternal evening falls
And it is like a dream between grey walls,
Between two walls of shrunken topless stone,
Between two walls with silence on them grown.
Here he stands, in a litter of leaves upon the floor,
In a solemn silver of scattered springs;
Among the smooth green buds above the door
He stands and sings.

This two-page black-ribbon typescript fragment (a version of "Orpheus," VIS *XII) differs considerably. While* VIS *XII is a dialogue (albeit imagined) between Orpheus and Eurydice, in this version only Orpheus speaks. (Photocopy. Photograph not available.)*

This fragment (a penciled holograph of "Love Song," VIS *IX, lines 60–74) is one of a series of holograph fragments of this poem. On the verso, not printed here, is a purple-ribbon typescript poem fragment containing elements of several poems in* Vision in Spring. *The typescript may be a draft fragment from the* Orpheus *sequence.*